Storm In A Glass

Of Water

A Small Town Story

VIVIAN SINCLAIR

Copyright

For news about recently published books by Vivian Sinclair and upcoming new ones visit Vivian's website at viviansinclairbooks.com

The Virginia Lovers Trilogy:

Book 1 – Alexandra's Garden

Book 2 – Ariel's Summer Vacation

Book 3 – Lulu's Christmas Wish

The Maitland Legacy, A Family Saga series:

Book 1 – Lost in Wyoming (Lance's story)

Book 2 – Moon Over Laramie (Tristan's story)

Book 3 – Christmas In Cheyenne (Raul's story)

Other books by Vivian Sinclair available on Kindle and in print:

A Guest At The Ranch, a western contemporary romance

Storm In A Glass Of Water, a small town story

A Walk In The Rain, a contemporary women's fiction novel

PROLOGUE

Hunters Crossing, Ohio
New Year's Eve

The house on top of the hill was like a beacon in the dark winter night. It had snowed the day before and the thin layer covering the ground was sparkling like diamonds. With all the windows lighted, the house was so picture-perfect that it resembled one of Thomas Kinkade's paintings.

Inside, the guests were gathered around the table in the dining-room waiting for the New Year to arrive. There was laughter and jokes, kisses, and champagne bubbling in crystal glasses.

One guest, a bit tipsy, raised his glass to his host and said, "Hey Charlie! It's time to make a New Year's resolution or wish …."

Charlie Callahan, the host, leaned back in his chair. "Hmm…a resolution…or a wish… A resolution would be to coach the high school football team to win the state champion title. …A wish….You see, my family and I, we are in good health. My boys are doing great. Rob is finishing college and was accepted to medical school. Drew is waiting for that football scholarship and applying to college. Then, my wife Lorena is as beautiful as she was the day I met her, and while we are not among the richest people in the country, we are pretty well set financially. So my wish for the New Year would be to keep things just the same."

Little did he know that the Fates had decided otherwise; to surprise him big time in the New Year to come.

CHAPTER 1

Charlie balanced the steaming bowl with popcorn and the icy beer in his hands and set them on the coffee table. With a groan of satisfaction, he sat down on the comfortable couch in front of the TV.

The college football game was about to start. It was amazing how much pleasure he had watching these games. Amazing - because Charlie was and had always been a baseball man. He had played baseball in the MLB for twenty-four years. Of course, he was no Babe Ruth or Cal Ripken. He didn't have their talent, fame, or money. But he had always been a good, reliable member of the team.

Three shoulder surgeries and the doctors' threat that he might not be able to move his arm if he continued playing professional ball, convinced him to retire four years ago.

Financially, he was fine, or even better than fine, because he had never spent his money on fancy cars or

3

expensive women, not even when he was very young. He graduated from college with a degree in financing and invested all his earnings in a diversified portfolio.

Now, at the age of forty-seven, retired in his small hometown of Hunters Crossing, Ohio, about an hour's drive from Cincinnati, the birthplace of MLB, Charlie was content with his life. He coached the high school football team and if sometimes he wondered if life had more exciting challenges to offer – well… he quickly stifled these thoughts. His life was good.

He was married to a beautiful and smart woman and had two great kids. Rob, the eldest was finishing college and had been accepted to medical school. Drew was finishing high school while pondering his future and trying to decide where to go to college. Of course, there was that one child who was lost to Charlie, but he had agonized plenty in the past about this. No more.

"Darn Robertson pass the ball…pass the ball to Sanders, he's free on the right…" Charlie almost choked on popcorn watching the blunder made by one of the younger, more ambitious players.

The couch dipped slightly. Charlie looked at his youngest son. "Ah Drew, I thought we'll watch this game together."

Drew seemed preoccupied by something else other than the football game on the screen. His nose scrunched like when he was a little boy and had thrown his milk out the window. Drew had always hated milk, especially lukewarm.

Charlie looked at him again. "Drew, what is it?" Then he smiled with understanding. "I know. You have a girl problem."

Drew was stunned. "A girl problem? No, nothing like that." He smiled too, full of mischief. "More likely you have a girl problem. An old girlfriend problem coming to haunt you."

"What are you talking about? I have never had any girlfriend while married to your mother."

"I know, I know," Drew tried to pacify him. "This was from your high school days. I think she called several times in the last two weeks and Mom tried to put her off. That you're not home, that you know she'd called, but you are busy – things like that. This morning I was upstairs and heard the conversation. This woman, Flora said that she only wanted to tell you something she discovered recently and that she was selling her mother's house and leaving Hunters Crossing for good."

"Flora, you say? Maybe… Floria. Pronounced like Gloria." Charlie smiled remembering the old times when he had been young and so much in love that it hurt.

"Yeah, Floria. Unusual name."

"After the main character in a famous Italian opera. Floria Tosca."

"How interesting!" Drew exclaimed. "I never heard of it. But then, I don't listen to opera too much."

Charlie laughed. "In this case, you haven't missed anything. It's one of those dramatic operas in which everybody dies at the end. Quite depressing. Give me a football game anytime." He pointed to the TV. "At least here the drama has a purpose."

"Did you love her?" Drew asked. "Your old girlfriend, I mean. Floria."

Charlie considered this. "I adored her. She was

everything to me. Of course, at the time I was a young naïve, seventeen year old boy, who didn't know any better."

"So what happened?"

"Her mother decided I was not good enough for her daughter and showed me the door. Let's not talk about it…"

"I bet she was sorry later, when you became famous," Drew said with indignation.

Charlie only shook his head. It was a bitter memory, humiliating, and full of pain. He could not explain to his son that people like Floria's mother didn't care about fame and money in professional baseball. She was too narrow-minded and snobbish.

"Did you meet her again? Your girlfriend, Floria?" Drew asked.

"No, she never tried to talk to me. She went on a date with my best friend, Jon. After a few months, we graduated from high school and she went to college in California. She never came to the Prom, although Jon had asked her. The way I knew it, she never came back to Hunters Crossing and her mother became a recluse."

"You didn't call her, Floria I mean?"

Charlie shook his head again. "Nope, I couldn't. There were no cell phones thirty years ago….And now it's pointless to get in touch, whatever her reasons may be. It's all water under the bridge."

"She seemed to be a nice lady and she needed to talk to you. I think you should call her."

"You think so?" Charlie's smile broadened. Sometimes his youngest son amazed him with his deep understanding of human nature. Charlie himself had been much more naïve and immature at the same age.

Drew nodded. "I think she needs to clear up the old misunderstandings in order to move on with her life, wherever she lives. And it might be good for you to listen to what she has to say." He took out of his pocket a tiny piece of paper and handed it to Charlie. "Here! This is her cell phone number."

The home team on the screen had scored a touchdown and Charlie was momentarily distracted, so Drew stuck the paper in his father's T-shirt pocket and quietly left the room.

CHAPTER 2

Lorena was late, very late. And today was a very important meeting of the Ladies Circle of Quilting and Gardening at the Country Club.

The Circle had been started thirty some years ago by Theresa Hunter, the only daughter of Dominic Hunter, who was a direct descendent of the Founder of the town. Unmarried, Theresa had been an avid quilter and a passionate gardener and as President of Ladies Circle, very influential in all the problems concerning the town and an active member of the Chamber of Commerce. When she died two years ago, the Mayor's wife, Wilma Jenkins, as First Lady of Hunters Crossing, had assumed the position of President of the Circle with the understanding that, as stated by Theresa Hunter, an election with all the members voting was to be held in order to elect a new president. That had been two years ago. Wilma Jenkins had postponed the voting indefinitely because the president of the Circle held an important position and real power, while the Mayor's wife was just a decorative figure.

Lorena was sure that she could beat Wilma in a real, honest vote because Wilma was not very popular.

Now, changing outfits in front of the mirror, Lorena had to decide what dress to choose. The problem was not which outfit looked better on her. The blue Nicole Miller dress fit her like a dream and the intense color complimented her blonde hair and blue eyes. By sheer luck, she had found it in her size in clearance at Macy's in Cincinnati.

The beige pantsuit was very elegant in an understated way and, with the suede pumps and the Michael Kors purse, looked very classy. Unfortunately, coupled with her white, true blonde complexion, it made her look pasty and washed out.

Lorena shook her head in regret. The desire to appear more subdued so as not to antagonize Wilma Jenkins won. She hung the blue dress back in the closet and went to look for the beige accessories. Soon, very soon – she promised herself – she would dress to look her best without trying to please or pacify someone who was hostile to her anyway.

Ding, dong!

Ah good! The Merry Maids were here. She could let them in to clean the house and then leave for the meeting. Maybe she would not be so late after all.

Ding, dong!

"I'm coming!" she shouted, grabbing her jacket and purse and going down the stairs as fast as her high heels allowed her. "I'm so glad you came on time because…"

Her words died in her throat as soon as she opened the door. Not the Merry Maids, but her scoundrel father-in-law, Billy Bob Callahan himself, stood on her front porch grinning like the proverbial Cheshire Cat, surrounded by four huge suitcases that had seen better days.

"It's good to be so warmly welcomed," he said and entered the foyer dragging after him two of his luggage.

"But... but I thought you were in Florida

romancing that wealthy widow," Lorena stammered in desperation.

"Yes, well, we had a disagreement and I thought that distance would make the heart grow fonder, don't you know," he said moving the last pieces of luggage inside the house.

Lorena narrowed her eyes. "You mean you put her money in one of your investing - get rich quickly - schemes. And she protested and threw you out."

He raised a hand. "Now see here, it was not like that. We had a disagreement and I thought to put some distance between us. That's all."

She tapped her foot. Billy Bob Callahan had been famous all his life for his ability to attract investors and to convince people that his schemes were valid and would bring a fortune. The fact that he truly believed in each and every one of them didn't affect the end result. Everybody lost the money invested, including him.

"How long do you intend to visit us?"

He waved his hand starting to climb the stairs. "Oh, a while…See how things go…"

"You can't do this to me Billy Bob. I was waiting for the Merry Maids and I'm late for the meeting and Wilma Jenkins will be so pissed and…," she wailed.

Now he stopped, dropped his luggage, and came back to her. "Why don't you go to your meeting and don't you worry. I'll take care of everything."

"But the Merry Maids…"

"Oh, I'll take care of them too. The more the merrier. No pun intended." He wiggled his brows.

"That's what I was afraid. It's a disaster." Lorena hiccupped.

He patted her back. "You are too stressed out. Seriously, go and trust me. I'll hold the fort here."

And so she went to her cute BMW, an indulgence from Charlie on her birthday, and drove the short distance to the Country Club. It was marvelous – she reflected – to have someone tell you: "Don't worry. I'll take care of everything." Even someone as unreliable as Billy Bob.

CHAPTER 3

Lorena tried to attract as little attention to herself as possible while getting into the spacious room at the Country Club where the Circle's meetings were held. The door made a squeaking noise and the empty chair near her friend Violet groaned in protest when she tried to sit down. So much for being unobserved.

Wilma Jenkins zeroed her eyes on her. "Mrs. Callahan! You finally honored us with your presence."

Lorena straightened her shoulders. She'd grown up in a poor part of town. Life had been rough there and she was a fighter. If you could not pacify them with niceties, then you had to fight them. As her Grandma used to say, 'If they pinch you, then you have to pinch back.'

In this case, no matter what she did, Wilma disliked her and tried to intimidate her. A spark of rebellion went through her.

Lorena looked back at Wilma. "We are not in school to be chastised for being late and treated like naughty kids. This is a meeting of friends who have common interests and who want to spend time together doing what they like and sharing stories or ideas. At least that is what Theresa Hunter intended."

Wilma opened her mouth, and then closed it like a fish out of water. Lorena had never objected so vehemently. She had opposed Wilma's ideas several times, but not openly defying her.

The awkward moment was saved by Molly Malone, the wife of a retired banker and a great quilter. "Lorena, my parents were so very pleased with the ideas you had for their anniversary. They wanted me to ask you if you would be willing to be more involved in organizing the whole thing, you know, renting a restaurant room, buying the food, flowers and decorations, that sort of thing. They wanted to hire a caterer from Cincinnati, but your ideas were so much better. It's their fiftieth anniversary and we, the kids, want it to be special for them."

Lorena was amazed. "You know Molly that I didn't do that kind of thing before….I don't know…"

"Not true Lorena," her friend Violet said. "Your own parties are splendid and you helped me with Annie's sixteenth birthday party."

"Oh Lorena," the lady near Violet asked, "could you tell me where did you order the magnificent cake with sugar flowers and butterflies that Annie had? And the lovely balloon arrangement?"

"I made the cake myself. Violet had a heart attack when I put it together and the top part almost fell over. She was there. About the balloons arrangement, I just picked some colorful balloons, ribbons, and silk flowers, and tied them in bunches," Lorena answered.

"It sounds simple, but you need a designer eye and imagination to achieve the right effect," Molly said again." I have an idea. My cousin wants to have a little party for her six-year-old son, nothing grand, so she thought of a pizza place. Her son wants a pirate party for his birthday, but she has no idea how to do it and she is a bit strapped for money what with her recent divorce. Could you organize something on a smaller size, cheaper?"

"Of course," Lorena answered. "Something nice can be done for every budget." Her mind was already imagining six-year-old pirates having fun around a ship-like cake.

"Well Lorena," Wilma's strident voice broke the image, "it seems you are in service. But then you should know how to do it."

The barb was referring at Lorena's mother, who had to work cleaning houses and doing laundry to support the family when her husband left her just after Lorena was born.

"Wilma, catering is a business," Violet interfered. "As for performing a service, so does a banker or a car salesman." Wilma's husband had been a car salesman before being elected Mayor. "Even the Mayor is performing a service to the community," Violet continued oblivious of the daggers flashing from Wilma's eyes.

"What about quilting?" Wilma asked still furious.

This time Lorena intervened, "About quilting, I have an idea. As you know, the Mayor is trying to find money to beautify the Main Street in front of the stores, to repaint the façade of the buildings, and to take care of the little green space in the middle. I think we ladies could pull together to donate quilts and other handiworks and to organize an auction, and the money could go to the city."

"Great idea!" Molly beamed.

"Wait a minute!" Wilma objected. "You think a few quilts and knitted scarves can solve this problem?"

"Not solve, but every bit helps," Mattie, an older woman, said. "I know Kevin from Bright Blooms nursery offered his work for free. The plant material, soil, mulch, and decorative containers cost money. The auction is a good idea."

The meeting was concluded. Lorena drove home partly exhilarated by the idea of catering parties and earning money doing what she liked, and partly worried that she'd aggravated the animosity Wilma Jenkins had towards her.

At home, instead of the chaos she expected, the house was clean and everything in good order. A very enticing smell of tomato sauce and herbs coming from the kitchen, guided her steps. At the counter, Drew was working on his laptop while laughing at something his grandfather said. At the stove, Billy Bob was stirring the tomato sauce in a pot.

For a short moment, Lorena was angry. Nobody messed in her kitchen. This was her sacred territory. Charlie and the boys never had the desire to cook or even to make a tea.

But the smell was divine and Billy Bob turned such a warm smile in her direction that she heard herself asking, "What herbs are you using, Billy Bob?"

"Ah, my special recipe for pasta sauce. Basil, oregano of course, and a little thyme and sage. Not too much to overpower the basil. Only a little to complement it." He smiled again. "But you must be exhausted. Come, please, and sit at the table. I have some fresh Jasmine tea for you." He was a charming rogue, a smooth talker no doubt about it. No wonder he convinced so many people to give him money for his crazy schemes. But she felt tired, so Lorena plopped down in a chair and let Billy

STORM IN A GLASS OF WATER

Bob soothe her with flavored Jasmine tea and feed her the most incredible pasta she had ever tasted.

CHAPTER 4

Charlie let himself in. The house was dark, but a nice aroma from the kitchen told him that Lorena was cooking Italian. One of his favorites. He climbed the stairs two at a time in a hurry to take a shower and change into the comfortable jeans he wore at home.

His cell phone vibrated. Not Floria again, he hoped. He didn't think Lorena would be happy to know he had contacted her, although there was nothing wrong with meeting an old friend to reminisce about old times.

He looked at the screen. Tony Darnell. Hmm! He had known a guy with this name several years ago, playing for the Orioles. He had been good, young, and promising. Then one day he had disappeared from the field. People said he was offered a big contract at ESPN. He was a talker for sure, but after that Charlie had never heard of him.

"Hello!" Charlie answered.

"Hi Charlie, my friend! How are you? I heard you retired a while ago." The jovial voice sounded as if they had parted yesterday.

"I'm fine. We all retire at some point. Some earlier, some later," Charlie answered evasively, wondering what could Tony Darnell want from him.

"Ah yes, yes. I want to talk to you about that. You see, for a couple of years now, I acted behind the scenes - so to speak. As a producer, director, and such. I do documentaries about sport, any sport, but my personal preference is baseball. So, a while ago I approached several people about doing a series of documentaries about baseball. Mainly great figures, traditions, like mom and pop going with the kids at the ball stadium. In a way, reviving America's love for this sport, considering that now many have turned their interest to football more than baseball. I finally have financial support and I'm starting to put things together."

"Great idea!" Charlie said. "But I don't see how I can help you."

"The people interested are at ESPN, but also the History Channel. And they suggested several names as narrator. At the moment, your name is at the top of the list. In other words, if you want the job, it's yours. Of course we'll need a speech sample, but from what we've seen, old interviews and such, you're what we need."

"Tony, I don't know what to say. You left me speechless."

"I understand. Why don't you take the time to think about it? Good money. We'll be based in New York. You have a month to decide, the sooner you let me know the better."

They hung up and Charlie dropped on the bed stunned. His first thought was to decline. What did he know of movies or television except to press the remote and eat popcorn at the right moment? Then he thought about his children leaving the nest. Rob had left already and Drew would leave in a few months. He needed to talk to Lorena about this.

CHAPTER 5

It was 5 in the afternoon at the Starbucks on Main Street.

Charlie Callahan was seated at a small table near the window, with his long legs folded like pretzels to fit under the table. In front of him was a cup filled with what the barista had called a skinny latte with some other stuff that he'd forgotten.

Charlie was a normal person who liked his coffee strong, black, and early in the morning. The barista, a girl who looked to be barely Drew's age and had several piercings in various places on her face, told him they had plain, black coffee, but wouldn't it be more fun to try something new. Because it was 5 in the afternoon and he didn't need the caffeine, he'd asked her what she suggested. And so, he got the skinny latte, with something else and caramel. She assured him it was coffee.

He took a tiny sip. It tasted like milk to him, only bitter and sweeter at the same time. He tasted it again.

Not bad.

Someone passed on the street in front of the window and seeing him nodded politely before walking on. Great. People would wonder what he was doing alone in the coffee shop without Lorena.

The door opened again and impatient, he turned. It was late and Floria was not here, although she had suggested this place herself. No, it was not Floria. This was a middle-aged woman, short, quite well-rounded and with short, blond hair. She made a beeline to the counter and ordered a Mocha, venti, decaf, non-fat, and light whip.

This last thing made Charlie cough to mask his laughter. The image of the woman in a red bustier with a whip in one hand and the coffee in the other was hilarious. How about heavy whip? He tried to take another sip of his latte, but to his surprise, the cup was empty. He had drunk it all without realizing it. Maybe he should get another, or maybe not. He checked his watch. Almost 5.30. He should leave.

Meanwhile, the woman picked up her coffee and

approached his table. Double great! Stood up by his date and on his way to be propositioned by a middle-aged matron.

She placed her coffee on the table, looked him over until he was blushing, and said, "Hello Charlie."

What! She could not be Floria. His Floria was young and beautiful, with long chestnut hair, reaching the middle of her back, wavy, glinting reddish in the sun, not this person with short, blond hair. His Floria was slim and with a sexy walk. All men looked at her when she passed by. If this woman moved like Floria she'd probably get a hip fracture. Her green eyes, beautiful and full of laughter … He could not see her eyes as they were covered with glasses. Stylish, but glasses were glasses and made one look like a grandmother, no matter how stylish.

Maybe it was better not to revisit with one's young love after thirty years, Charlie reflected. One should keep only the memories of youth, beauty, and love. The reality could be depressing. Discreetly he patted his hair. Was it a bit thinner on top?

"Charlie, I wanted so much to see you before leaving."

Wait! The voice. Charlie closed his eyes. The voice was like he remembered. Melodic and almost singing and her laughter like little bells. So uniquely Floria.

She grabbed his hand over the table.

"I know you might think it's stupid. It's been thirty years and it's all water under the bridge. We've moved on and have families and lived different lives, but..." She sighed. "The way we parted was... not right. My mother died recently and I came to Hunters Crossing to sort everything left in the house and sell the house before going home. I live in California now."

"I know, I heard," Charlie said. Perhaps he should say he was sorry for her loss, but he would be lying. He doubted anybody who knew her mother was sorry. The old woman had been a mean, selfish, and manipulating person.

Floria shook her head. "I know it doesn't matter now but I just found out that she lied to me. Remember the last day when you were supposed to come to pick me up to go to the movies?"

"Yes." He remembered it as if it had happened yesterday. "She told me you were upstairs and didn't want to see me and I should go and never come back. That you had grand plans for your life that didn't include me." He remembered and it hurt almost as much as thirty years ago. Maybe now the humiliation was a stronger memory than the pain of losing Floria.

"No, no Charlie. She sent me to buy something and when I came back, she said you hadn't come. I waited and waited. She implied that you don't care for me anymore. It's such a cliché situation. Like Romeo and Juliet. You feel like smacking them over the head. Why didn't they try to talk to each other before jumping to conclusions? Why didn't we talk to each other?"

"Because my father and I were changing residence quite frequently and had no phone at the time. Cell phones didn't exist. Besides, shortly after, we left to college."

Floria took off her glasses and rubbed her eyes.

Her beautiful green eyes. "For a year after that, I used to walk to college every morning with tears in my eyes. I was mourning losing you. Why didn't we try to communicate?"

"Me, because my pride had been injured and I felt humiliated. I believed your mother that you had plans that did not include me. That I was not good enough for the mighty Hunter-Clark family," Charlie said.

"Nonsense. My mother had illusions of grandeur, but you knew me. I was not like her."

"Well, it might have been also the fact that you went on a date with Jon, my best friend at the time."

"I went on 'one' date and that was to ask him about you. He didn't tell me that my mother chased you away," Floria said with sadness.

"Of course not. He was in love with you, with hopes of his own."

She seemed surprised. "You know – and this explains also why I didn't try to find you and confront you – I was very insecure. I mean I knew boys liked me but, because both my parents didn't love me and my mother always put me down, I believed that I could not be loved."

Charlie was stunned. "You were one of the most attractive girls I met. Pretty and warm and sexy. All the boys in high school wanted to date you."

She looked at him with tears in her eyes. "That's so nice of you to say. Thank you."

"So what did you do after that?" he asked.

"I went to college at UCLA, as far from Ohio as possible. Then I looked around me and picked the most promising boy in the class and in two years I got married despite my mother forbidding me to marry. I never came back until now. The marriage didn't work out. We split up a few years ago, but I have a beautiful daughter, smart, with a PhD in Chemistry." She said with pride in her voice. "What about you? I mean I know a little about your life from small town gossip and of course I know you played baseball in MLB."

"I had a pretty good career playing professional baseball, but in the beginning I made a mess of my personal life before I met Lorena twenty-five years ago.

Now I'm retired."

The young barista approached their table. "Hey guys, can I get anything else for you?"

Floria looked at her, then at her watch. "Oh Lord! It's almost closing time. Where did the time go?"

Outside, she turned to him, "Thank you for meeting me. I needed to talk about this. I'll be in town for some time, for a couple of weeks, until I finish sorting all the stuff and list the house for sale. You know where I live. It would make me happy if you want to visit. I need a friend," she confessed shyly.

"Sure. I'll come," Charlie said, not sure this was a good idea.

She rose on her tiptoes and kissed him on the cheek. "Thank you."

CHAPTER 6

Lorena was balancing the upper tier of the cake, trying to fit it on the base tier without mishap. It was the anniversary cake for Molly Malone's parents. This was the most difficult step, assembling the whole cake. Two tiers plus two doves on top. A bit tacky if you asked her, but it was a special request from the man who called his wife 'my dove'.

When she had looked online and then asked Mary at the bakery shop, she discovered that it was a pretty popular decoration for wedding or anniversary cakes. Easy to make from sugar paste and Marzipan once you had the moulding.

Billy Bob was hovering nearby holding the plate with the base tier steady. To her big surprise, not only had he been a big help with all the cooking and planning for the party, but also he had actively encouraged her that she could do it. "Do you want me to dress in black pants and white shirt to serve the guests? You need a waiter and let's not waste money hiring other people," he said.

"No. It's true that I just started and don't have money to spend. We'll set the food made by us, the aperitifs and the cake, on the table. The entrees will be served by the restaurant. I would like you to act more like a host, guiding people in, tempting them with the food on the table, answering their questions, that sort of thing. Could you do it?"

"Absolutely. Talking to people is my natural talent," Billy Bob assured her.

Lorena shook her head. "Billy Bob you are not, I repeat NOT to force any of your schemes on them or I'll be very mad. You have to swear this to me."

He looked at her like a deer in the headlights. Also he seemed hurt. "I swear. This is your business and I'm not going to interfere. I only want to help."

Lorena smiled at him. He was hurt. "Thank you. You have been a great help to me."

Ding, dong!

First she tried to ignore the bell ringing.

Ding, dong!

She set the top tier on the table and wiped her

hands.

Ding, dong!

No use ignoring it. "When the bell is ringing, it means the person at the door wants something," she said.

"Maybe it's a friend…"

"Nope. A friend would send an email or a text-message or simply call my cell phone. This persistent person either wants to sell me something I don't need, or wants to convert me to the Church of Latter-day Saints," she said going to the door.

On her front porch was an elegant young woman, probably in her twenties. Although dressed in jeans, those were 200 dollar jeans. Lorena knew her designer jeans and the faded blue color came from special treatments, not from too much washing. The soft lilac pullover was cashmere and the oversized purse casually hung on her shoulder was Coach. Expensive chick. Not a blinds salesman, nor a Latter-day Saint.

"I would like to see Charlie Callahan," she said. A small tremor in her voice betrayed the fact that her confidence and poise were an act.

Great! Lorena thought. She had to fend Charlie's old girlfriend's phone calls for two weeks and now a younger one was looking for him in person. And this one was trouble. "Charlie is not at home," she said preparing to shut the door.

The other one stopped her. "I would like to wait for him. I just drove from Virginia and I need to speak to him," she said pointing to her Lexus.

She was not from Hunters Crossing for sure. Here everybody knew everybody else and his business. This girl was not from around here.

"Very well," Lorena said opening the door wider. "Come in. I hope you don't mind if we go into the kitchen. I'm somewhat busy."

"Not at all. I like kitchens and this smell of vanilla and butter cream is great." For the first time the girl's smile was genuine, nothing forced or socially polite. "I'm Amanda Forrester by the way. I'm from the Washington DC area. I live in Falls Church, which is in the Northern Virginia side of our Capital."

"Nice to meet you. I guess you know me since

you knocked on my door. I'm Lorena Callahan, Charlie's wife. Where did you meet Charlie?"

"I didn't… Meet him that is…That's why I came. To meet him"

Lorena stopped and turned around in the kitchen door. "Who are you and what do you want with my husband? You'd better tell me right now."

The girl hesitated and raising her eyes to Lorena said, "I would prefer to tell this to Charlie."

Lorena narrowed her eyes. "But you'll tell this to me, because by law Charlie and I share everything including the trouble you're bringing."

"Oh no! I don't want to create problems for anybody."

"Who are you?"

"I'm Charlie's daughter."

CHAPTER 7

"Whaaat! What do you mean?" Lorena's high pitched cries made Billy Bob pop out of the kitchen to see what the ruckus was about. Lorena continued in the same tone, "I was married to Charlie for twenty-five years, since he was twenty-two. He hasn't…"

"And I'm twenty-seven," Amanda interrupted softly.

"Why don't we all go into the kitchen and I'll make some tea," Billy Bob suggested.

"Your darn tea is not going to solve this problem." Lorena turned to look at him. "Billy Bob did you know anything about this? Did Charlie know?"

Amanda stepped into the kitchen and took a seat at the table. "Yes, Charlie knew. Let me tell you first that I didn't come here to cause mischief or to disturb your family life. I am a lawyer and I have my career in Washington DC. I don't want money; I have my own. All I want is to meet Charlie. I have never known him and if you ask me 'why now', it's because I have recently discovered that my mother had deceived me when she told me he'd never wanted me or that he didn't want to be involved in my life."

"You really are his daughter?" Lorena asked.

Amanda nodded. "As you know if I were lying a simple DNA test would tell the truth. Charlie was nineteen and my mother twenty-six when they met in Chicago. They spent a week together and then he left. I understand his baseball career was just starting and he left for Baltimore I think. My mother told him as soon as she discovered she was pregnant. Charlie refused to marry her. At nineteen and with his strict schedule of training and hard work to build a name in baseball he had other priorities. He promised to support her financially and asked to see me. I found this out only recently. My mother was delusional to think he'd marry her. Angry, she refused his request to see me and told me that he didn't want me."

Billy Bob shook his head. "And you believed that Charlie will abandon his child. He's not that kind of man."

"I didn't know what kind of man he was until a month ago when I discovered a bunch of letters hidden in the drawer of an old desk. In short, he had paid a generous child support of his own free will and not enforced by any legal process. My mother had always complained how difficult it was to live only from her income as an accountant. When I was eighteen, he stopped the payments, but he paid my college and then law school tuition. My mother had claimed she'd taken loans to cover the amount that was not covered by my scholarships. There were also unopened letters for all of my birthdays," Amanda said rubbing her eyes.

"He had hired a lawyer to explore the possibilities of getting at least visitation rights, but your mother argued that this will disrupt your life and be detrimental to you," Billy Bob said.

"You knew about all this?" Lorena turned to him.

He nodded. "Yes, but it was not my story to tell. Besides, Lorena, what good do you think this would have done? Charlie was unhappy enough about the whole thing."

Amanda pointed a finger at the kitchen island. "That thing is going to topple over."

Lorena jumped from the chair. "Oh, my cake! Billy Bob let's crate this thing."

They adjusted the supports for the second tier and Lorena placed the doves on top and they fit the whole tower in the special box.

Amanda watched fascinated. "I've never seen such a beautiful cake in my life. Do you think they'll have the heart to cut into it?"

Lorena laughed. "Of course they'll cut it and eat it too. It's pretty good if I say so myself. Billy Bob, do you mind driving the SUV to take the cake to the restaurant? And please watch them when they unload it and store it in the refrigeration unit."

"Don't worry. I'll do that." He gave a jaunty salute, and then turned to Amanda. "By the way, I'm Billy Bob, in case you didn't know. That makes me your grandfather."

Amanda clapped her hands. "I have a grandfather, how great. For so long it was just my mother and me."

"Wait to see your rascal brothers. Then we'll see if you want more family," Billy Bob said. "All right. Let's go to work. We have a party to run."

Lorena was less inclined to be gracious or to accept her into the family. Discovering her husband had a secret daughter that he never told her about was a bitter pill to swallow.

And so, when Charlie came home late that afternoon, except for the new Lexus in the driveway, the house was quiet and nobody was there.

At the Bella Serra restaurant in town, the party was a success. The decorations and flowers were admired, the food was enjoyed, and the guests oohed and ahed over the cake and the doves before demolishing it and proclaiming it to be the most delicious cake they ever had. Billy Bob charmed everybody and they thought he was a distinguished guest, not part of the catering team. Amanda had fun playing the waitress and helping Lorena.

When Charlie came downstairs, he found the three of them sharing a bottle of champagne to celebrate the start of Lorena's catering business. The meeting between father and daughter was anticlimactic. Amanda was exhausted at the end of this long day, she'd already told her story, and the champagne made everything fuzzy. She even wondered if perhaps she had not come looking only for the father missing from her life, but also for a whole family life.

Charlie, while happy to unexpectedly meet his daughter, a moment he'd fantasized for so long, was somewhat overwhelmed by this grown-up, beautiful woman. His dreams were off. He could not spoil her by buying pretty dolls, nor could he take her in his arms to the zoo and explain to her about animals. If she were a boy, then he'd talk about baseball and from there they could become more at ease and tackle the past. But this confident, beautiful woman confounded him and made it more difficult to approach her.

To top it all off, Lorena was mad at him for not confessing the whole thing. He tried to explain that talking about this was painful to him, but this was not enough to appease her.

CHAPTER 8

It was Friday afternoon and the high school stadium was full of people shouting and clapping, encouraging the local team, the Hunters of Hunters Crossing who were playing against their arch-rivals the Knights of the neighboring Clarksville. Parents, relatives, friends, and classmates were gathered to offer support to their team. Unfortunately, it was the 4th quarter and the Knights were leading 23 to 6.

It was one of those days when everything that can go wrong went wrong, Charlie thought. First, the previous afternoon, Colin helped his father Ken, from Ken's Auto Shop and Towing, to lift a car on the towing truck bed when he slipped and wrecked his knee. Colin was one of the best quarterbacks the town ever had and without him there was little chance to succeed in the offensive. He swore he could play, but his knee was swollen and the doctor advised against.

As if this were not enough, today at lunch, JJ, their defense star, was challenged by a classmate to eat three of the largest hamburgers at Burger King. JJ ate them all and now he was sick as a dog, running to the bathroom every ten minutes. His replacement, a very enthusiastic but skinnier kid, was flat on his back in the field, pushed by the Knights offensive.

Charlie had to admit that even Drew had a bad day, missing his cue most of the time without any particular reason. Charlie covered his face with his hands. He peeked through his fingers in time to see Drew missing another pass and the Knights grabbing the ball and scoring a touch-down. It was a disaster. Finally, the end of the game put a merciful end to the agony of seeing the score difference increase.

People emptied the Stadium fast, no doubt eager to put the memory of this game behind. Charlie left his jacket on the coach bench and climbed the stairs to the exit to catch his friend Victor and ask him if they were on for tomorrow's golfing. It was cold and Charlie regretted not taking his jacket. Victor disappeared before Charlie could reach him.

He turned back when he heard a strident female

voice saying, "Drew Callahan was a disaster. We have better players, but he is kept on the field because of who his father is."

Upset, Charlie turned and said, "You don't know what you're talking." The voice belonged to a thin, tall female looking down her long nose at him, or trying to, considering that he was taller. In her hand she had a large cup of brown liquid, probably soda. Her friend, to whom she was talking, was shorter and glancing desperately to the parking lot, now almost empty, where a car was honking.

"Of course I know what I'm talking," the acidic voice continued. "Drew Callahan is sissy and gay. He shouldn't be part of the team. He's a disgrace."

At first, Charlie thought he'd heard wrong. She couldn't talk about Drew like that. Then the anger made him see red. She had no right to talk like that about Drew, bad day or not. "Shut up, you ugly old biddy!" he shouted.

Her mouth snapped shut, but the hand holding the drink raised and she threw the soda in his face, drenching him in liquid and bits of ice stuck to his now wet t-shirt. The shock from the contact with the icy drink made him raise his hand and in a reflexive gesture pushed her arm away. The cup fell to the floor and the woman emitted a shrill cry.

"Help! He assaulted me. Help!" Her friend who was on her way to the parking lot came back, but otherwise the Stadium was empty. "Officer! Officer!" At the gate, a police officer charged with the security at the game was ready to go. Hearing her cries, he approached them. "Arrest this man, officer!" she demanded. "He assaulted me."

The officer, a tall, burly man, with coffee colored skin, took out a notebook and started writing. "What exactly happened here?"

"He assaulted me, I told you. You should arrest him."

The officer looked at Charlie who was drenched in soda, drops of liquid hanging on his eyebrows. "How did he assault you?"

"He pushed me. He slapped my hand."

"Was that before or after you threw the drink at him?" he asked. Charlie was frozen and unable to think or say something. He knew he should explain but felt unable.

The woman lost her patience. "Before, after, what does it matter? He should be arrested. Instead, you're interrogating me."

The officer kept writing. "I can't arrest a man without documenting the case." He turned to the other woman. "How about you ma'am? Have you witnessed the events?"

The other woman looked at her friend then shrugged. "Actually, I was closer to the exit. My husband was impatient to go. Wilma here was telling me that Mr. Callahan's son, Drew was not good at football and he made the team only because of who his father is. And Mr. Callahan told her that she didn't know what she was talking about. That's all I saw and heard. But if Wilma said he was aggressive, I'm sure she is right," she said with a look of loyalty to her friend.

The officer sighed and turned to Charlie. "What

about you, sir? Do you agree with what the lady has said?"

Charlie shivered, but succeeded to find his voice. "Yes, it was like that."

"And then?"

"Then she" – and Charlie pointed at the first woman – "she told me that my son is gay and has no right to be in the team."

"And it is the truth," the woman called Wilma said, "and he told me to shut up and called me unspeakable things."

"What did you call her?" persisted the officer, writing in his notebook.

"I called her 'an ugly old biddy'." The officer's corner of the mouth twitched like he was trying to contain his laughter. "And then she threw her drink in my face and instinctively I pushed her hand away from me and she dropped her empty cup."

"I see….Do you agree this is how it happened?" the officer asked Wilma.

"Yes. He pushed me and called me all those

names. You should arrest him."

The officer sighed and closed his notebook. "Tell you what, folks. It was a difficult day, with the local football team losing the game. We all are a bit tense because of that and people are upset and agitated. I understand how these things can happen. How about we all go home and cool down. I'm sure tomorrow we'll see things differently."

"What? I demand you arrest this man, officer," Wilma cried.

"I can't do that, ma'am. You both said words and both were aggressive." The officer tried to pacify Wilma.

Wilma narrowed her eyes and asked him, "What is your name, officer?"

"I'm Officer Tramontana with Hunters Crossing Police Department."

Increasingly agitated, Wilma pointed her finger at him: "Officer Tramontana, let me make myself clear. If you don't arrest this man, you might not have a job tomorrow. Do you know who I am?"

The officer stiffened. "I know who everybody in

this town is and I'll pretend I didn't hear you threatened me. Go home ma'am."

"I'm also a descendant of Thomas Jefferson."

The officer shrugged unimpressed. "And I'm a descendant of the Pope."

Wilma stamped her foot and left, muttering threats, followed closely by her friend.

"A descendant of the Pope, huh?" guffawed Charlie.

"Could be. Pope Borgia had eight or ten kids. My papa is Italian from Calabria."

Charlie looked at him. "You don't look very Italian if you don't mind my saying so."

The officer smiled. "That is because my Mama is a southern belle from New Orleans. Now, you better go and change your t-shirt before you catch a cold. Have a nice evening." He saluted and left.

CHAPTER 9

Charlie needed to talk to someone, to be understood and soothed. So he went to see Floria. Her house was a beautiful old Victorian, located in an older, more affluent neighborhood. At least that was what he remembered. He hadn't been there in thirty years; since the day Floria's mother had thrown him out, telling him he was not good enough for her daughter. What hurt the most was that even if he were to succeed in professional baseball and achieve fame and money, he would always remain a worthless, stupid jock, unworthy of her daughter. This had robbed him of the complete satisfaction that he had succeeded in life. After every game won or being praised in the news, a little part of him remained discontented, thinking that this would not have been good enough for Floria and her social circle. Not that he had ever needed their acceptance, he only had wanted Floria to be proud of him and consider him worthy.

It was possible that this episode with the Mayor's

wife brought back the memories of being judged and considered part of a lower specie. It brought back old insecurities that he'd thought he was mature enough to overcome.

Approaching Floria's neighborhood, he felt his heart beating faster and anticipation mixed with a remnant feeling of unease. Once, this was THE place to live in Hunters Crossing. In time, things had changed, as did everything else in life. Where once had been the trailer park to the east of town near Silver Lake, very modern condominiums had transformed this area into a desirable, gentrified neighborhood with great views of the lake, manicured landscapes, and all the amenities.

Charlie himself lived on the west hill, where a few years ago a developer from Cincinnati took advantage of the panoramic view and built several larger houses on generous lots. This was considered now the best - or 'posh' as the British like to say – part of town.

Floria's street, bordered by huge oak trees, had some splendid examples of classic architecture, Victorian, Arts and Crafts, even some more modern Art

Deco houses. No cookie cutters here. Most were well preserved, but not all. Floria's house, very beautiful from a distance, showed signs of neglect when Charlie drove closer. The walkway to the main door had cracked concrete and weeds peeked through the cracks. The gingerbread was discolored and the whole house could use a coat of paint. The roof was covered with patches of moss. It was sad, Charlie thought, to see the decay, but maybe the future owners might restore it to its former glory.

He knocked on the door and Floria, dressed in yoga pants and an oversized t-shirt opened the door and looked at him in surprise. Maybe he should have called. But she smiled and grabbed his hand and pulled him inside. "Charlie, how wonderful that you came." She beamed at him and just like that all his doubts and worries vanished. She dragged him to the kitchen, a small, square room, completely separated from the living quarters. No open concept floor plan in these Victorian houses.

"Tea or coffee?" Floria asked him.

"Tea, please. It's late for coffee." He looked around him. The décor was unchanged from the way he remembered it.

She placed a plate with cookies and a mug of fragrant tea in front of him. "I know you like the chocolate chip ones, but these are fresh, sugar cookies, made by Mrs. Murphy this morning. Try them!"

"Do you bake, Flori?" Charlie asked, feeling more mellow in the warmth of the kitchen.

She laughed. "I cooked and baked all my life, but not anymore. I'm alone and there is no point in cooking only for myself. Now, tell me what bothers you. Because I feel you need to talk to someone."

Charlie told her. Amazing how easy it was to unburden and confess it all. His worries, his problems, his doubts. All. While Floria, her hands wrapped around the now cold tea mug was listening, looking at him with her expressive, big green eyes. He told her about his youthful folly and yearning to see his little girl. And now when she'd finally come to see him, he didn't know how to talk to her, how to reach her, afraid he'd say or do something wrong, afraid he'd lose her again, this time forever.

Then he told Floria about this minor, stupid incident with the Mayor's wife which left him upset and with a bitter taste because people could be so mean sometimes and lash out in anger and hurt the others.

Floria took his hands across the small kitchen table. "Charlie dearest, about Amanda it's very simple. You have to talk to her with honesty about all that happened. She already knows the facts. You only need to explain things from your point of view. Then, you have to stop thinking about the past, which cannot be changed, and to concentrate more on the present relationship you can have with her. I mean, yes, she found out recently that you didn't abandon her, but it might be more than just the desire to meet you. She might have some difficulties of her own and no one to turn to."

Charlie froze. "Oh my God, Flori, do you think she's in trouble? She said she is a successful lawyer in Washington DC. I never thought to ask if…"

"No, no…," Floria interrupted him, "I didn't

mean she is in trouble. I just thought that she might have problems, professional, personal, any kind, like everybody has and she would like or need to talk to you. That's all. Don't panic."

He breathed deeply. "Not in trouble. Okay. Still you are right. I should talk to her, ask her about…things. And if she's upset by my questions, too bad. That's what parents are for, to be annoying, nagging, and to butt in where they are not wanted."

"True. That's how you treat your sons, isn't it?" Floria sighed. "About the incident with the Mayor's wife, I know you said it's not important, but I heard – and Mrs. Murphy is very well informed – that Wilma Jenkins can be a difficult person and people avoid to get into a conflict with her. Just be careful in dealing with her."

Charlie shook his head. "I'm sure it was a silly incident. Everybody was upset that the team lost the game. People say things. It's just… I don't know…"

"It was because she said Drew is gay. That's what bothers you."

"No, of course not. She just said so because she

was mad. A nasty woman. It's ridiculous. Drew gay…
How could she say that?" Floria just looked at him.
"What? You don't think Drew is gay, do you?"

"Calm down, Charlie. I don't know him. I talked
to him once. That's all. I think he is a very sensitive and
caring young man. More than others his age are. If he's
gay or not, is not the issue here. Maybe he's not sure
himself yet. He's what? Seventeen? Well okay, at
seventeen he probably knows. But, my suggestion is to
try to talk to him about his problems, plans, intentions,
life in general. I think he might be torn between doing
what he thinks everybody expects of him and what his
personal preferences might be. Is he close to his
mother?"

"Not any closer than he is to me," Charlie said.
"He used to talk to Rob, but since Rob left for college,
not so much. I saw him talking to Amanda several times.
I mean talking, not just joking around."

"That's it, just go and have serious talks with
both your kids and you'll feel much better, you'll see."
And Floria kissed him softly on his cheek, hugged him,

and sent him on his way.

CHAPTER 10

They were all gathered around the table having dinner. Lately, this was not happening very often. Lorena was busy with her blooming catering business and it seemed Billy Bob was very much involved in it too. With no one to cook dinner, Drew made a passion for take out pizza or Thai food. The family room was littered with empty boxes. Thank goodness for the Merry Maids cleaning the house once a week.

"Amanda, you've been so much help, arranging the platters, and talking to the irate florist yesterday..." Billy Bob said, cutting into his steak, grilled to perfection by Charlie. "I hope you have more vacation. We could use your help a little longer."

Lorena set her fork on her plate and looked at Amanda. "How long do you plan to stay with us? Can you take time off from you busy attorney job?"

Amanda's attention seemed to be on the pieces of broccoli she pushed around on her plate. Finally, she sighed and said, "I don't know if you guys follow politics. Drew does, I know that." She smiled at Drew who nodded encouraging her to continue. "It was in the news recently and at CNN a story about Senator Edgar John Smith."

"Aha," remembered Billy Bob, "the one caught by his wife in his office, after hours with some other woman in a compromising situation."

"Yes, he was not only caught, but also the wife took pictures and posted them on Facebook. It was a scandal and nobody supported him after that, not only because he had run on an honesty and integrity platform, but because the other woman was aide to a senator from the opposite party. He had to resign."

"Okay, but what does that have to do with you?" Lorena asked, as she was not following politics on CNN. "My God, you were not the other woman?"

Amanda laughed. A spontaneous burst of laughter. 'Thank you Lord.' Charlie thought. A newly found daughter involved in a public political scandal was not what they needed. They would be one hundred per cent behind her, supporting her, but it would be better not to be in such a situation.

"No, not at all," Amanda continued. "I was however one of his political advisors and once he resigned, our jobs were finished too. So I thought I should take some time off to think about what direction my career will take."

"You can stay here as long as you want and if you need any help from us you have only to ask. You are part of this family," Charlie said, not looking at Lorena for approval. This was not negotiable. He intended to help Amanda any way she needed and he was glad to have her live with them.

"Oh Charlie, this is so nice of you to offer," Amanda said smiling at him. For the first time there was no reserve or caution when she looked at him. "Fact is I have several options. Washington political world is quite small, as in 'everybody knows everybody and his business'. We have to, in order to be able to negotiate and reach agreements. I have four job offers; two to join other political teams, one position on a committee at UN in New York and the last one, to join a lobby firm, which

I know I'm not going to do. In addition, I am a lawyer and I can work anywhere I want independently. So you see I'm not exactly without perspectives. I only need to take a step back and decide."

Later that evening, Charlie knocked on Drew's door. Drew raised his head from whatever he was doing online. Probably posting on Facebook. Nowadays, one did not sneeze without posting pictures of the event on Facebook. Charlie felt old. Lorena was in charge of periodically posting family news and pictures of the family. Charlie had no time and he valued his privacy more than writing a diary for all to see when he got drunk.

He sat down on Drew's bed. Drew turned around to face him. They had always had an easy relationship. "Hey Dad, what's up?"

Charlie told him the whole after game story.

Drew stopped fidgeting with his pen and looked straight at Charlie. "Are you asking me if I'm gay?"

Thank you Flori, for pointing out what was

important, he thought. "No Drew, I'm not asking you that. You'll tell me when you'll feel you want to. I only wanted you to be aware of what happened and that some people can talk more than they should. Now what about your college applications. Did you decide where you want to go?"

Drew looked at him and scrunched up his nose. He was worried about something. Charlie wanted to hug him and protect him and take the worries away, like he did when Drew was a little boy.

"Dad, Amanda is a blessing. When I felt so confused and alone, she encouraged me to just be myself and think of what kind of life I want. She's great Dad." Charlie flinched. He was proud of Amanda, but also a bit hurt that Drew didn't come to him to talk. "Anyhow," Drew continued. "It's like this. I am gay. I like football, but not enough to play it in college and I'm sorry to disappoint you, but I decided not to go to Ohio State. I was accepted to the prestigious Rhode Island School of Design and I think I'll accept."

"I didn't know you applied to Rhode Island…,"

was all Charlie thought to say overwhelmed by all this news. "I'm not disappointed in you. I could never be. It's just unexpected, I guess…All this…You want to do design? Very interesting…Hmm…"

Drew laughed. "No Dad. Not design as in fashion design. I draw political cartoons and it seems my drawings have been appreciated. I have a blog that is quite popular."

Charlie listened to all this with astonishment. It seemed there were a lot of things he didn't know about his son and for the first time he felt inadequate as a parent. "Look Drew, I'm not a pathetic old man, but I am in a way old-fashioned… That is to say … I don't approve or disapprove of gay people. Frankly, I didn't care one way or another…It was not affecting me or my family, so in a way it was not important."

"Oh, but it is…"

"Yes, well, so is world peace, but I'm not going to solve it myself. Sorry! Poor choice for a comparison. Anyhow, what I wanted to say is that I loved you since you were born. You were so serious and tentative before doing or trying something. Rob was more impetuous, jumping in before considering too much, and falling on his feet most of the time. You were my little boy and I want to assure you that no matter how muddled my mind is right now, I will always love you and support you in any decision you make for your life, personal or professional." Charlie left the room quickly to take care of the allergy that was making his eyes tear up and before saying more stupid things.

CHAPTER 11

Charlie had considered the after game incident minor and was very surprised a few days later, when he was served papers to be present in court in front of Judge Rollins to answer Wilma Jenkins' accusations that he assaulted her. He threw the papers on his desk, frustrated with the woman, but still not considering this a big deal. Then it crossed his mind that Judge Rollins was golf buddy with Mayor Jenkins, but he figured once he told the truth, the whole nuisance would go away.

He'd forgotten that, Hunters Crossing being a small town, gossip was an important part of everyday life and people talked and took sides before knowing the whole truth. He found this out a little later in the afternoon when he heard the front door and Lorena's voice.

"Charlie! Charlie come down here. NOW!"

Oh no, Charlie thought, she'd wrecked the BMW again. At least she was not hurt. Not if she could shout so loudly. And Charlie sprinted down the stairs.

"Charlie how could you?" Lorena wailed.

How could he? Not the BMW then. He hadn't touched that car.

"No need to pretend you don't know what I'm talking about."

She'd found out about Floria, innocent as that relationship was, Charlie thought.

"You assaulted Wilma Jenkins," Lorena continued in the same shrill tone, her hands on her hips, a sure sign that she was mad. Otherwise Lorena would never do it, the posture being considered vulgar and Lorena was very careful of her facial and body positions, often studying them in front of the mirror; this smile, that profile, or hand gesture. Everything needed to be perfect.

"Now listen …" Charlie said, pulling her into their pristine white living room where nobody entered except the Merry Maids with their magic cleaning wands. "…what is this about? Do you truly believe I assaulted this woman or any woman ever? Do you?"

"No, of course not." She shook her head. "I know you didn't, but I'm angry that you let yourself become embroiled in such a situation and with Wilma Jenkins of all people. Everybody in town will believe her, not you. I hope you realize that."

"Come sit down and tell me first why you are so afraid of this woman."

Lorena hiccupped and wiped her tears with the back of her hands, another indelicate gesture that escaped her control. "I heard it today at the Ladies Circle of Quilting and Gardening…"

Charlie's jaw dropped. "Ladies Circle of… What on earth were you doing at …"

"What? You think I'm not good enough to be part of the Ladies Circle. Let me tell you that I would be elected president if the Mayor's wife, who assumed the role of temporary president, would let the members. But she won't let us vote, 'cause she's afraid to lose. And now she's trying to make me look bad. Violet heard her saying that I'm white trash from the trailer park area of the town. And now this…assault thing."

Charlie raked his fingers through his hair. Things were more serious than he thought. "First let me tell you that I think you are TOO good for this Circle. You are a great person, mother, wife, and now successful entrepreneur. Where you were born or raised is irrelevant. It is remarkable that you have overcome difficult conditions. Why would you consider attending this boring Circle for old, gossipy women, is beyond me. Quilting? Really! You never liked to sew, not even a button. It reminded you of your mother, all the time patching things. You don't even knit, not quilt."

She smiled. "True. I don't like to sew or knit for the matter. Not to mention sewing buttons. All those buttons that the boys used to lose and I had to replace. Ugh! I'll tell you a secret. I don't quilt. Violet does and we pretend that we are doing a project together. I suppose at home she needs to undo all that I mangled."

"Then why? Why do you take part in this Circle? And gardening? We do have a wonderful garden, but we have also a wonderful gardener who takes care of things. I'm sure I heard you saying that you don't like to plant flowers."

"True," Lorena admitted. "I hate getting my

hands dirty in the soil, with bugs, slugs, and worms. Disgusting. I like to cook and having my hands clean is essential. I wash very well all the produce I cook. Even mushrooms and any cook knows that generally it is recommended not to wash them 'just pat them dry because if you wash mushrooms they become rubbery', " she mimicked. "I wash them thoroughly before cooking. Do you know how much dirt and bacteria gather on their surface? How can one ignore that and cook them unwashed?"

Charlie scratched his head. Was a headache coming? "I don't know about mushrooms, washed or not. I still don't understand why you are wasting your time with all these things you don't like."

"Because the Ladies Circle was founded by Theresa Hunter and many of the issues discussed at the Circle were later implemented as decisions in the Chamber of Commerce of the city. It's all about prestige and power, Charlie. Why do you think Wilma Jenkins doesn't allow elections? She's afraid she'll loose."

"Are you telling me the president of this Circle is

some kind of Queen of Hunters Crossing?" Charlie joked.

Very serious, Lorena nodded. "Something like that. You may laugh Charlie, but at this level, in Hunters Crossing, this is what is important. We live here, in this small town, and with the prejudices and people's tendency to look down their nose at the others in order to feel superior. People like Wilma Jenkins and her followers. We have to play by their rules Charlie. Please promise me you'll fix this situation."

"I promise. I will fix it. You can be sure of that," Charlie said.

CHAPTER 12

Next day, Charlie got a frantic call from Floria who, well informed by Mrs. Murphy of all the goings on in town, needed to know if he was all right.

"So you see, dear Flori, no need for you to be worried," Charlie concluded his story of yesterday's events, from his perch on the chair, in her bright yellow, warm kitchen. He took a sip of his tea, looking around. The décor was a throw back to the avocado decorating era, mixed with some remaining Victorian items like the cabbage pink roses, quite faded, but still recognizable in the wallpaper border near the ceiling.

"Of course I'm worried, Charlie. Something needs to be done," Floria said, placing warm cookies near his mug of steaming tea. These were chocolate chip cookies, his favorite.

"If you tell me that I should make nice to that woman, while she's insulting my son, I'll be real mad with you, Floria, and disappointed," Charlie mumbled, between bites of the heavenly tasting cookies. "I'll explain it all to Judge Rollins and that will be the end of it."

"No. No, to all of the above. No to making nice, whatever you meant by that. And are we talking about Judge Rollins, the same one who plays golf with the Mayor at the Country Club? Charlie, you have to be serious and fight," Floria said, waving her small fist in the air.

"I had no idea you were such a bloodthirsty girl," he joked, his mouth full of cookies.

"No jokes, Charlie Callahan. You need a lawyer," she said pointing her finger at him.

Charlie considered this. "I guess I could pay a visit to the offices of Weinstein & Krantz."

Floria made a face. "Are we talking about Jacob Weinstein who was lawyer in town thirty years ago? He used to come courting my mother, when in reality he wanted the house. This house. Ugh."

"He retired, but Jacob Jr. is a carbon copy of the old dad."

"Any chance the Krantz in the company is

better?" she asked.

"Not really. Krantz is cousin to Jr. They are the only lawyers in town. I don't think I should go to the trouble to hire a lawyer from Cincinnati for this small problem."

Floria took a dainty sip from her own tea mug before answering. "Go see Weinstein and if you're not impressed, call me. Weinstein is not the only lawyer in town."

A huge neon sign announced that the big building right in the center of town on Main Street, belonged to Weinstein & Krantz, Attorneys-at-Law. In the parking lot to the side of the building, two almost identical black Mercedes cars announced how successful the said attorneys were. Charlie's blue Ford truck was quite out-of-place in such company.

At the reception desk, a very young woman was talking on her cell phone. "And I told Bobby, why should I wait until you consider the right time when…" She paused, looked Charlie up and down, and then spoke into her phone, "I'll call you back in a minute." She placed her cell phone slowly on her desk and in a bored tone asked, "Do you have an appointment with Mr. Weinstein?"

"No, I don't. But I'm sure he'll see me," Charlie answered amused by her antics.

He was sure she'd have pointed him out, if not for the opening of the inner door and the appearance of Jacob Weinstein Jr. himself.

"Wendy, I needed the other file…" The girl jumped from her chair to give him the right file in the same instant Weinstein saw Charlie. They had never been close friends, but they knew each other from the Country Club.

"Charlie," he said, his face stretching with a big smile that didn't reach his eyes. "How are you? Please come into my office." He turned to his receptionist. "See that we are not disturbed."

Weinstein gestured for Charlie to take a seat in the chair in front of the desk and then he closed a small cabinet, but not before Charlie could see several bottles of whisky and French Cognac. "Now then, what brings you here?" Weinstein asked and he took a seat in his own executive leather chair behind the desk.

When the lawyer turned his flinty eyes and phony smile on him, Charlie understood that this was not friendliness. This was not his friend and regardless how small the issue was, he'd go to Cincinnati or further to find a lawyer whom he could trust. "Thank you for receiving me, Jake. I need a lawyer and before looking in other places I thought I'll ask your opinion." Now, Charlie was sure a refusal was to come.

Weinstein measured him before answering in an even tone. "Before you say more I want to warn you that our office's services are already engaged by Mrs. Mayor Jenkins."

"Ah!" Just as Charlie expected.

"A very distressful affair, this. Very distressful."

"Very distressful indeed," Charlie repeated. "But the way things evolved I don't think I'm going to accept Mrs. Jenkins apologies for the insults to my son and me."

With this said, he stood up and left, but not before

looking at Weinstein, who remained at his desk, mouth open, speechless. He smiled. Not many people could say they left an attorney speechless.

His satisfaction was short. Bottom line, he had no attorney and he was not naïve. He realized Weinstein was a force in court. The best attorneys in Cincinnati might be too busy to take his case seriously and would also not know the people in Hunters Crossing and the intricate relationships in this small town.

Depressed, Charlie drove back to Floria. She pulled him into the kitchen and eyes brilliant, without asking what happened, she said, "I have the right person for you."

CHAPTER 13

Charlie walked slowly along Main Street, looking for a lawyer office, other then Weinstein & Krantz. That was what Floria had said, 'office on Main Street'. He looked around. Nothing. He walked back again and stopped in front of Starbucks.

The door opened and a person with a cup in his hand exited and they almost collided. "Victor!" Charlie exclaimed. Victor was Violet's husband and Charlie's friend and golfing partner. In the last years they had been at each other's house for birthdays, anniversaries, barbecues, or for no reason at all, just being friends.

Victor nodded curtly and crossed the street. Charlie stood there dumbfounded. What was that? Yesterday, a guy he knew from the Country Club pretended not to have seen him and looked the other way. But Victor? He didn't remember offending him in any way. And if so, he could have complained or something. Charlie shook his head, looking into the narrow alley, opening from the outdoors space used by

Starbucks'customers in summer. It was kind of a hidden alley. And then he saw the sign: Michael Fraser, Attorney-at-Law.

He stepped with care between two iron tables piled with chairs on top and got in front of the small building behind Starbucks. The sign was lighted in the window. Two rickety stairs led to the door. Charlie knocked, but nobody answered. He tried the handle and the door opened. He stepped into a large room with stairs on one side, leading upstairs. Charlie looked around. Boxes of all sizes, opened and unopened were piled on every inch of space, on the floor and on the furniture. To the right, two, very nice glass French doors led to another room, also filled with boxes everywhere. No receptionist or any other person could be seen around. Where they in business? Oh Lord, where did Floria send him?

"Hello! Anybody here?" Charlie asked, starting to feel like Rebecca in the DeWinter mansion. A damsel in distress from a gothic novel.

Some noises could be heard from under the mahogany antique desk. Charlie pushed the boxes to the side and on the floor, and from under the desk popped up a Harry Potter look-alike head, red hair though, but the same round glasses.

'What are the chances this is the receptionist or the boy in charge of unloading the boxes?' Charlie asked himself.

Meanwhile, Harry Potter extricated himself from under the desk, smiled and put out a not so clean hand for Charlie to shake. "Hi! I'm Michael Fraser. Nice to meet you!"

After a brief hesitation, Charlie shook the hand, wondering how to explain that it was all a mistake, that he was just passing by, and he was not in need of a lawyer.

"Please, take a seat!" Michael continued in the same cheerful voice.

Charlie looked around again and proceeded to move the boxes from the chair on top of those already on the floor.

Michael sat on the boxes. "You are my first client. Isn't it great?" His smile was huge. Well, at least he was honest and genuinely pleased.

Oh dear Lord! Jacob Weinstein will eat him alive, Harry Potter glasses and all, Charlie thought. "Did you at least finish Law School?"

"Huh?" Michael looked at him nonplussed.

"You said I'm your first client."

"Sure. The first in my practice in Hunters Crossing. Didn't Cousin Floria mention this?"

"No, she didn't," Charlie said, feeling sad that Floria recommended this guy.

Michael smiled again. "Before you tell me your problem, let me tell you a little about myself. I think it will help if we knew each other better. I finished Law School at Yale, eight years ago. I've been hired by Stone, Moscowitz, and Stone immediately afterwards, because I interned with them before. If you are not familiar with them, I can tell you that this is the most prestigious law firm in Philadelphia. I worked there eight years, doing everything, mostly criminal, but other stuff too when necessary."

"Criminal?" Charlie gulped.

"Criminal cases, but all sort of other cases too. It was exciting and I was well on my way to become a partner when I realized I had no life except my work. Even sleeping had become a luxury. It was a sure path to burn-out. I decided to change pace and move."

"You got to be kidding me! Yale. Moscowitz and Moscowitz." Charlie wondered if this was a dream. "Nobody educated at Yale, with a promising career in Philadelphia moves to Hunters Crossing."

Michael smiled again. "You did. Not Yale, but great career, money and all."

Charlie opened his mouth, and then closed it. Then he said, "I was born here and when choosing a home base it seemed like a good idea." After a brief pause he added: "You know there are no criminal cases here, unless you want to consider mine. The most exciting professionally will be to wrestle an estate settlement from Weinstein."

Michael laughed. "I don't need to wrestle him. They'll come to me directly."

Then under all the good-natured laugh and Harry

Potter glasses, Charlie saw the keen intelligence and determination to succeed, the confidence and power to best the others. "Do you know Jacob Weinstein?" he asked.

Michael inclined his head. "I do, yes. He's not going to be a problem in any way. And Krantz is spending most of his time in Florida."

Charlie decided that Floria was right again. This guy was a force to be reckoned with, especially because he looked unassuming and people would underestimate him. Charlie decided to trust him. "Okay, let me tell you about my situation and then you'll decide if you want to take my case."

"To paraphrase you, Are you kidding? You are my first client here. Of course I'll take your case. Besides, Cousin Floria will tan my hide if I don't. You've been strongly recommended."

Charlie told him the whole story and Michael kept writing on his laptop and bugging him with all sorts of details that Charlie considered unimportant, but what did he know. He added the story of the Ladies Circle for

Quilting and Gardening and the presidential election dispute, just because he considered it funny. Michael however seemed to think it was important and typed all the details.

When Charlie finished his story he felt incredibly relieved, a big weight taken off his shoulders. "What do you think?" he asked Michael at the end.

He got the familiar smile. "Piece of cake," Michael said, rubbing his hands, excitement in his eyes, like a horse ready to start the race. "And I'm not saying this because I'm a bragging sort of vain guy. I'm a professional and I know the rules of this fight better. In other words, Weinstein is good, but I'm better."

"Do you know also that Judge Rollins is playing golf with the Mayor?"

"Yes, I do. But he's no pushover and… will see," Michael finished.

Charlie looked at him. "In all fairness, I have to warn you that many people in town prefer to humor the Mayor's wife and to see me as the bad guy. Even my good friend, Victor avoided me, although he'd known me for years." Michael started writing again and Charlie continued, "You being new in town and all, I have to tell you this. Being on my side will make you less popular and you'll get less business."

"Let me worry about this. Because by the time I'm done with this case, the people in Hunters Crossing will beg for my business. No bragging, only the truth." He grinned.

CHAPTER 14

It was early in the morning and the air was crisp. Charlie felt invigorated by today's practice session. The boys were in very good shape today and the passes were flying from one to the other. Even Drew was working with his teammates very well. No more distracted looks and missed catches. The second coach, the PE teacher was also very animated, running all over the place shouting directives not all the time the right ones, but the team was oiled and acting as one.

Satisfied, Charlie called for five minutes break. "You guys were good today," he praised them. He always did, regardless of the outcome of a game. Smiles and high-fives answered his praise. "If the game were to start this minute I have no doubt you would smash the opposite team. Now small break and we're on the field again."

Charlie went to the bench and got out his water bottle from his duffel bag. He was checking his cell phone for messages when Pablo, the school janitor approached him. Pablo was a wizened old man and doing this job for ages. No one could remember when he had not been here or remember him as a younger man. Now, he had a frown on his already creased face.

"Coach! Himself, Mr. Murphy wants to see you now."

'Himself Mr. Murphy was Donald Murphy, a pompous, self-important, short man who happened to be the Principal of the Hunters Crossing High School. He was also vaguely related to Floria's neighbor, Mrs. Murphy, who didn't seem to hold him in high esteem. He was also an active member of the Country Club. He and Charlie were saying 'Hello!' when meeting, but nothing more. Charlie avoided his company mostly because every time the other saw him, he tried to straighten his posture and look down his nose at Charlie. This was laughable as Charlie, a professional athlete and in great shape was a head taller and very fit. Murphy's round belly didn't help his image no matter how he tried to suck it in.

"I'll finish practice and go, Pablo," Charlie said,

wondering what the Principal's displeasure was today.

The janitor shook his head. "Himself said 'Now' and he was mad. I feel trouble on the horizon, Coach. Mark my words. You better go now."

"All right. I'll go now," Charlie agreed. No need to create more problems for this old man. If Murphy wanted a fight for whatever imaginary grievance or real resentment he had, Charlie was ready.

Ignoring the secretary's invitation to wait outside, he knocked briefly and entered Murphy's sacred office. "Hello Don!" Charlie said.

The Principal was standing behind his desk, looking out the window. He didn't turn to face Charlie.

"Well Don, if the problem is not an emergency, then I'll go back to the team. Pablo might have misunderstood," Charlie announced, after waiting ten long seconds for the other to acknowledge him.

Murphy spun around. "You!...You!" he sputtered pointing his finger at Charlie. Then he recovered his usual pompous manner and said gravely. "It has come to my attention that you, Mr. Callahan have assaulted, verbally and physically a delicate lady." He paused to add more importance to his words. "This is not tolerable in this place of education, in this high school." He was gaining steam in his speech. "We have to set an example to our students and to protect them from bad influences."

Charlie smiled grimly. "So much for, 'innocent until proved guilty' or 'listen to both sides of the story before judging'. Who told you all this? The delicate lady, I presume."

The Principal pointed his finger at him again. "You are fired. Effective immediately."

Charlie lost his patience. "You can't fire me. I'm not an employee of the high school."

This seemed to leave the Principal confused. "But you are a coach at the school."

"I'm not a PE teacher. Man, don't you know to whom you pay a teacher salary? I'm not on your roster. I only offered my services as a coach on a volunteer basis, so to speak."

"Then you are fired from offering your services any longer. Please leave the school's premises." The

Principal recovered his aplomb.

Charlie was so mad, he turned to leave. When he reached the door however, some little devil pushed him beyond limit and he said, "You know, Don you shouldn't always listen to rumors and make hasty decisions based on them. A rumor is like people hearing you making weekly trips to Cincinnati and hiring services of women of ill repute."

The Principal opened his mouth like a fish out of water. "You…you don't…know…," he stuttered, visibly shocked.

Charlie opened the door. "Sure I know. A delicate lady told me."

CHAPTER 15

It had been a petty revenge to leave the Principal speechless and to have the last word, Charlie acknowledged. The second person in as many days. This however didn't change the facts. Things were not looking bright, not at all. He would soon be a pariah in his own hometown. In fact, this was what that hateful woman wanted. Not going to happen, but he was weary to have to fight people he considered friends, neighbors, and close acquaintances, people with whom he had shared happy moments. He would win in the end, but would it be a pyrrhic victory?

He was walking to his truck in the school parking lot, which was almost empty at this hour, when he heard barking. A small, dirty dog with scratches on his ear sat near his front wheel, waving his little tail and giving short barks of welcome at Charlie. He bent to scratch behind his uninjured ear. He was a mutt of undetermined breeding, kind of ugly and still cute in a way. He probably had fleas.

STORM IN A GLASS OF WATER

When he was a little boy, he had wanted a dog, but Billy Bob nixed the idea. He had trouble taking care of Charlie, and a dog would have been too much, he said. Later Charlie was on the road and in training most of the time and Lorena decided dogs were bad for allergies and their mostly white décor was not conducive to having dogs. Rob brought a stray home when he was in middle school, but after a couple of months the dog disappeared and Rob went on to other hobbies that kept his attention. Charlie wondered what had happened to that dog.

He opened the door to his truck. The dog stayed where he was near the front wheel. "Look, I had a bad day and I have to go. You go where you came from. I don't want to hurt you by accident. Now shoo!... Go!"

Nothing. The dog stayed put right there, near Charlie's truck, waving his stubby tail, his head leaning to one side and looking at Charlie with expectation. "You go there." Charlie said pointing vaguely to the other side of the parking lot. Nothing.

Not knowing what to do, Charlie stepped two parking spaces to the side and said, "Here! Come here!"

pointing to the spot near him. And miracle. The dog came right away. "Sit!" Charlie ordered and the little dog plopped his butt right there where Charlie had pointed. "You stay here," he commanded once more.

He went back to his truck, opened the door and climbed behind the wheel. The dog stayed where he was ordered. Charlie started his engine and backed carefully out of the space. He was almost out of the parking lot when he looked in the rearview mirror. The little dog remained where he was ordered, looking after Charlie, his head cocked to the side, trying to understand the game they were playing. Darn, the idiot dog had probably been trained to obey. He might stay there until night, waiting for Charlie. Someone could hit him.

Charlie pressed on the brakes hard and the truck stopped with a screech of tires. Charlie opened his door, turned his torso and leaning out called to the dog. "Hey Scruffy! Come here!" The dog ran like a bullet from a pistol, jumped with much agility for one so small, right in Charlie's lap. He swiped his tongue over Charlie's cheek. "Ugh."

STORM IN A GLASS OF WATER

The dog stepped onto the passenger's seat and plopped his behind there looking forward. He turned his head to Charlie, gave him the canine equivalent of a grin and looked forward again almost saying, 'Let's go! What are we waiting for?'

Great. He was unemployed, half the town mad at him, and now a scruffy dog was his responsibility. All in a good day's work, as they say. What to do with the dog? He was trained, which meant he might have a master. Did he run away? He looked like he'd been in a fight with a thorny bush and lost. He might be hurt.

Charlie knew the vet in town. Doctor Leonard Wiseman. While they were not good friends, Charlie and the vet had partnered a few times on the Golf Course. A nice enough fellow. A few years, maybe ten, older than Charlie. This was it. The vet would know what to do with a stray dog.

Charlie searched his phone for the vet's office address and let it guide him driving there. The parking lot was full. Charlie barely squeezed his truck into a narrow space. He got out and the dog jumped down right after him. Charlie worried that without a leash he'd lose the dog before even talking to the vet. No such thing. Charlie said, "Scruffy, come!" and the dog marched right near him.

Charlie, with the dog at his heels stopped in the door of the waiting room. Chaos reigned inside. Three dogs of various sizes, barely restrained by their masters, were barking and jumping trying to reach a marmalade cat, who was hissing at them perched on the shoulder of a pained-looking woman. All the people were speaking at the same time, competing with a parrot, who was talking loudly from the arm of an older man. "Hit him, hit him, kill him," cried the parrot. Or something similar.

Charlie was afraid that Scruffy would join the fray, but the dog sat at Charlie's feet, raising his eyes to Charlie for guidance.

A door opened and a young woman, in a white lab coat, with a ball of white fur in her arms came out. The tag on her pocket read: Dorinda. She approached a middle aged matron and gently placed the little ball of fur on her lap. "Mrs. Henderson, Fifi here had been such a good girl when Dr. Wiseman administered her vaccinations. You should be proud of her. She was very brave."

"Oh my poor Fifi," wailed the woman like she herself had been given the shots.

The little white dog, who had a tiny pink bow on top of her head, settled in the woman's ample lap.

Scruffy cocked his head with interest.

The young assistant, named Dorinda, looked at Charlie and smiled. "How can I help you? And who is this handsome fellow?" she asked.

"Hi! I'm Charlie Callahan and I found this dog half an hour ago in the high school's parking lot. I don't know anything about him. He might be lost. I couldn't leave him there. He could have been hit by a car or …" Charlie said.

The woman patted Scruffy gently on the head. "Let me talk to Dr. Wiseman."

After a couple of minutes she returned. "The doctor will see you now."

Charlie looked at the others in the waiting room,

but nobody protested or paid attention. When he entered the office, Scruffy with him, the veterinarian came to welcome him with a smile, which surprised Charlie. Or maybe he was not 'au courant' with the latest news in town. "Charlie, I haven't seen you in ages. And who do we have here?" he asked looking at Scruffy.

"I just found him and I think he's lost and I don't know what to do…"

"Let's first do an examination," the vet said. "On this table, please."

Scruffy looked at Charlie. "Up, here," Charlie commanded and the dog jumped up immediately.

"Very nice. Obedience school. I'm impressed," the vet said. "He's not one of your everyday stray dogs, although his breeding is not clear. And he looks unkempt," the vet continued to talk while moving his hands gently over the dog. "He's a boy, already neutered, not here, not by me, or I'd have remembered him, no ID tags, collar or electronic. I also know that in the last days nobody mentioned a lost dog, not here or at the Humane Society. He probably had vaccinations, but I'll repeat them just to be sure." He then stopped his hands and stiffened. "When did you say you found him?"

Charlie peered more closely at Scruffy. "About half an hour before coming here, in the school parking lot. Why? What's wrong with him?"

The vet sighed. "I'm sorry but this little guy had been abused. He has some welts on his skin, under his fur, not entirely healed."

With a dreadful feeling Charlie said, "I hope you don't think I…"

"Lord! Charlie, of course not. Only look at him! He adores you. Do you think I can not distinguish after all these years of practice, obedience enforced from fear and obedience willing to please. This dog decided you are his champion. He is loyal and the abuse was not long enough to break his spirit. Look at his eyes, clear, playful, following you. Not shivering with fear." The vet laughed. "It looks like you've been adopted Charlie."

Charlie raked his hair with his fingers. "No way, Leo. Lorena will kill me if I come home with this dirty dog. Can't I take him to the shelter?"

"You could. But I hope you are aware that if he is not adopted by somebody, in ten days, two weeks max, then he'll be put to sleep. They don't have enough space and volunteers as it is, which is a shame."

"Put to sleep?" Charlie repeated horrified. Even Scruffy whined in protest. Not possible. He didn't save the dog only to let him be killed at the shelter. "No way," he said. "I'll take him."

"Good. Great." The vet rubbed his hands. "He'll be good for you. You'll see. I'll prepare all the paperwork, electronic ID, and a collar and leash. Nothing fancy. You'll have to go to the mall. How long has it been since you've been to the mall, Charlie? There is a PetsMart there and you can buy everything necessary." He placed a few things in Charlie's hands, including a booklet, thick enough to put to sleep a whole classroom of students. The vet continued, "Here you have a list of all necessary items. While you shop there to your heart's content, in the back of the store they have a groomers' business. Treat the dog with the luxury package. You'll not recognize him."

STORM IN A GLASS OF WATER

Charlie opened the booklet and turned a few pages. He felt dizzy. Who knew having a dog required so many things to buy, to do, to know.

The vet attached Scruffy's collar and leash and handed it to Charlie. "He's young, not a puppy, a year or so old. You'll not regret taking him in. Trust me on this, Charlie."

"Easy for you to say. You don't have to face Lorena. I hate to think what she will say."

The vet patted him on the back. "I'm sure you have your way to convince her." He went back to writing in his computer. "What name shall I put here?"

"Mine. Charlie Callahan. I'll pay for this exam."

The vet laughed. "The dog, Charlie. The file has the name of the dog."

"Aha!" Charlie nodded. "Scruffy." The dog looked at him.

"Scruffy? You can't be serious. It's not dignified. Dogs have their dignity. Besides soon, after grooming he'll be a real handsome dog. Come on!"

"What would you consider a dignified name?"

asked Charlie.

"I don't know. Beethoven. You know that movie about a dog…"

"Does he look like a Beethoven to you? No, thank you. Scruffy fits him, a bit rakish and…"

"Okay, okay, Scruffy it is. Now go and treat him at the groomer."

On his way out, he heard Leo Wiseman say, "Are you free by chance this Saturday for a round of golfing, Charlie?"

"Sure, I am," Charlie answered. He didn't add that he was free now everyday, not having his coaching position any more.

"I'll see you at the Country Club Saturday morning, around 10."

CHAPTER 16

After an hour of shopping and three trips to his truck with stuff deemed 'absolute necessity' by the salesperson at PetsMart, Charlie thought he might need to trade his truck for a bigger one to accommodate all the needs of his newly acquired dog. He went to the groomer who presented him with his dog, all his hair fluffed up, smelling like a field of blooming flowers in spring.

"Scruffy?" Charlie exclaimed in wonder.

"No, sir," the groomer replied offended. "He is not scruffy at all. Except for this scratched ear, he looks very civilized. Maybe you would like to attach a bow, near his ear, covering the worst."

"No bow, he is a boy."

"A blue bow?"

"No bow at all. It might confuse him." Not that it mattered, Scruffy being neutered.

"Well then, this is all we could do," the groomer said.

Charlie assured him he was very pleased with the

results and paid his bill leaving a substantial tip that mollified the groomer.

At home he entered with some trepidation, holding Scruffy's leash. Not that the dog needed one in the house. He was very well behaved.

"Charlie!" Lorena shouted from upstairs.

He sprinted upstairs, Scruffy keeping pace with him.

Lorena was in the small sitting-room off their large bedroom, her red-rimmed eyes a proof that she had cried. "Do you know what happened today?"

He did, but did she?

"There was a meeting of the Ladies Circle of Quilting and Gardening and Violet called to tell me she'd heard Wilma Jenkins telling the others that she wanted to exclude me from the Circle as I come from a family with no morality," she wailed.

Charlie clenched his fists. He was not a violent man, but when his family was attacked he was ready to strangle that vicious woman. "And what did you do

Lorena?" he asked, deceptively calm.

She raised her eyes to him. "Nothing. I couldn't bear the humiliation. I didn't go. You promised you'll fix it Charlie."

"And I will. I got a very smart lawyer and we'll face the Judge soon."

"But Charlie, I thought you'll go talk to her, pacify her somehow…"

"You thought that after she insulted our son and me, falsely accused me of a crime, sued me and terrorized you, I'll go to apologize to her? This is what you thought of me? Besides, do you think that a simple apology is what she wants?"

"What does she want, Charlie? Why all this malice?"

Charlie shook his head. "I don't know if she has a special reason or she is just a bully whose viciousness spiraled out of control. But I promise you when the fight will be over she'll regret she started all this and she'll never be able to harm anybody, not in this town."

"I want to believe you, Charlie, but when will all

this be over?"

"Soon. Trust me." He bent to kiss her.

Lorena sniffed, looked at him and sniffed again his shirt. "Charlie, you smell…where have you been?"

"And if I've been near a charming, nice smelling lady, what would you do?"

"Scratch her eyes out," she answered promptly.

Charlie smiled. This was his Lorena. "Good news is that there was no lady, charming or otherwise."

"And the bad news?"

Laughter and cries of delight from the hallway meant that Amanda and Drew had discovered Scruffy.

"Scruffy! Come here boy!" Charlie said and the dog came running and sat near him.

"Charlie, what is this?" Lorena asked.

"This is Scruffy. The source of the flowery fragrance that you smelled on me."

"Did he pee on my carpet and you doused him in Febreze?" Lorena asked.

"Certainly not. He's very well behaved and trained. The smell comes from the groomer. Think - Spa for the ladies."

"Whose dog is this?"

"Mine," Charlie answered.

"You thought that we don't have enough problems and brought a dog home on top of all…" Lorena complained.

"No, I didn't think. It happened. And I'm keeping him." There were very few instances when Charlie didn't humor Lorena. This was one of them. She sensed it in the finality of his voice.

"Just keep him out of my kitchen," Lorena told him. "The first pee on the carpet and he's out," Lorena warned him. She turned to look out the window. "Oh Charlie, what am I going to do?"

"Does this Wilma thing affect your business? Did you loose potential customers?"

"No, no. The business is going well. Amanda and Drew designed a great website with pictures. I put adds and other pictures online and got business from the neighboring towns too."

Charlie nodded. "Good." It still bothered him that

Lorena, so fierce in facing other difficulties in life was so vulnerable when confronting bullies. She cracked in front of adversities that Charlie considered unimportant, like what other people think. She dissolved in tears because she might not be accepted in the high society of Hunters Crossing. "God Lorena, do you want to be the queen of Hunters Crossing?" He laughed remembering a previous conversation.

Very serious she said, "Yes Charlie, that's exactly what I want. I was born dirt poor in the trailer park. I worked hard to improve myself and this is what I want. There is nothing wrong to want to be better, to be on top."

Charlie sighed. "Then, my girl, we have a problem because I don't have the same ambition. Different priorities in life, I guess."

CHAPTER 17

Saturday morning was sunny, although a bit chilly. It was a perfect day for golfing. Charlie enjoyed the physical activity and Leo Wiseman's company. Strange how they've never been closer friends before, maybe because Charlie had never had pets and so they had no opportunity to talk more.

"Ah! A birdie!" Charlie exclaimed.

The vet was not paying close attention and Charlie turned to see what happened.

Leo elbowed him and said, "Do you think she's trying to break her legs or training for a walking on stilts competition." In front of them, advancing through the mown grass was Winona, administrative person at the Country Club, or some such. Nobody knew what was her exact job description, including herself. She was tottering precariously on five inch stiletto heels, which were not very stable on concrete or hardwood floors. On uneven grass they were an orthopedic surgeon's reason for living. Half way to them, one of the heels got stuck in the ground and she had to hop around trying to dislodge it. The two golfing partners admired the view, considering that this year very short skirts were in fashion.

"Do you think that flash of bright pink is her petticoat?" Charlie asked.

Leo laughed, covering Charlie's eyes with his hand.

"Hey!" Charlie protested. "What about you?"

"I've been single for the past seven years. I can look."

When Winona reached them, she fluttered her long eyelashes, gave them a view of her impressive cleavage, and then addressed Charlie in her throaty voice, "Mr. Callahan, Dr. Mahoney would like to talk to you. Could you please come to his office?"

She was pleasant on the eyes, Charlie thought, and he was appreciative of a feminine figure. "I'll finish this game…"

"Dr. Mahoney needs to go to Cincinnati, you know. Today is Saturday."

Charlie didn't know what Saturday had to do with

Cincinnati, but he excused himself to Leo and followed the tottering siren to the Club's main building placing a hand on her lower back from time to time. To help with her balance, of course.

Edgar Mahoney was the President of the Country Club. Why he called himself Doctor was a mystery. He was not a medical doctor for sure and neither had he a PhD. Otherwise he was quite an unassuming kind of man, mostly listening to others.

He greeted Charlie, offering his hand and inviting him to sit on the chair in front of his desk. He looked through the papers on his desk, sighed and looked back to Charlie.

"Mr. Callahan." He had always been very formal, so no surprise. "We have a problem."

What problem, Charlie thought, he'd paid his dues this year to the Country Club, quite a hefty payment.

"A big problem," Mahoney continued. "As you know, every member of our Club needs to have a sponsor. The sponsor's letter needs to be renewed every year. In your file the letter for this year is missing."

Charlie would bet the other distinguished members didn't bother renewing each other's letters every January 1st. "I'm sure Victor forgot to write it."

"We tried contacting him, but he didn't return our messages." Mahoney peered at him over his dark framed glasses. "And," he said in the same monotone, "we have rules and regulations we are obliged to follow. So,…you are excluded from the Country Club, Mr. Callahan."

Charlie was stunned. "I'm excluded because Victor forgot to write the letter. What about my having paid the fee for this year? Doesn't this mean I am a member?"

"Unfortunately, the dues are non-refundable."

"But the letter could have been misplaced."

"Could have been, true," Mahoney conceded. "But the end result is that you, sir, have no sponsor's letter. The rules and regulation need to be followed. You are excluded, sir. Good day."

If he didn't suffer a stroke now, then he'd live to be a very old man, Charlie thought. "If you are such a stickler to rules and regulations, Mahoney…."

"It's Dr. Mahoney, please."

Charlie was very angry. "I'm not going to ask to see your doctoral degree, Mahoney. I'm only going to tell you that for the sake of the rules and regulations, that you are so fond of, you, sir, should have paid the rent you owe for this building and the Golfing Club. The rent is in arrears for three years and many certified letters, demanding that the rent be paid, have been ignored. How would you feel if I told you that the Country Club is excluded…from the premises for failing to pay rent? Rules and regulations, you understand."

Well, this was the third person who threw him out recently, only this time Charlie was determined to do something about it. He joined Leo, who was exercising his swing and explained why he could not continue playing. First, Leo was dumbfounded. He'd never heard a similar story in twenty some years since he'd joined the Club. Then he promptly offered to write a sponsor letter on the spot for Charlie.

"Thank you, Leo. Your friendship means a lot to

me. But we both know where this situation originated and I have to take care of it myself."

"Yes, you have to. If nothing else, for the kids on the football team who can't play without your coaching." Leo hefted his golfing bag in his SUV. "You know, Charlie, as a member of the Club I'm entitled to bring a guest golfing. Consider yourself invited anytime."

Charlie laughed. "That would be a riot. Thanks. I'll think about it."

At home, the aromas coming from the kitchen almost knocked him out and reminded him he'd had no breakfast this morning. Lorena's high pitched voice and Billy Bob laughter meant that there was a catering affair being prepared in his kitchen and not his breakfast, or lunch, or whatever meal. He was not picky.

Upstairs, Scruffy, who resided now in his office, welcomed him like his long lost twin brother.

Charlie searched in his desk drawers, got a folder with some papers and grabbed the leash, to Scruffy's delight. "Yes, boy. Sorry for abandoning you this morning, but now we're going out." First he drove to Starbucks and bought himself a warm Panini sandwich and a latte. Scruffy had been fed doggy food in the morning and was not interested in the sandwich. He pulled on the leash toward the alley.

"Hey, how do you know where we're going?" Charlie asked him, while devouring the Panini. He considered going back for another one, but the cat Scruffy was following with determination, entered through the barely cracked open door at the attorney's office.

Inside, the same chaos of boxes was everywhere. No progress in unpacking them was visible since the last time he'd been here. Scruffy, cat forgotten, was looking for a place to lie down and finding none, he looked at Charlie.

"Michael!" Charlie shouted, moving boxes around to create a space on the carpet for his dog.

"Yes, where is it burning?" Michael answered, coming down the stairs.

"I need a cutter," Charlie said, unloading some

books on the empty shelves behind him.

"It should be there, on the desk where you left your coffee cup." Michael studied the cup with interest. "I should go and buy one for myself too"

"Not before we finish the business," Charlie said throwing two thick books on the shelves.

"Hey, careful with those. They are 'International Commercial Law'."

"I'm sure you can't survive without International Commercial Law here in Hunters Crossing," Charlie replied opening more boxes and folding the old ones. "Where shall I stack the empty ones?"

"Um…I'm not sure." Michael was busy getting acquainted with Scruffy and the dog basked in all the attention and scratching and petting that he got.

Charlie gathered all the folded boxes and decided to hide them under the stairs.

"Wow!" Michael exclaimed after looking around him. "The room is …empty."

"Now, let's talk business!" Charlie sat in the armchair, in front of the recently filled bookcase and opened the folder he'd brought from home.

Michael brightened. "Yes, I got another client, a very respectable Mrs. Murphy who wanted to write a new will."

Charlie raised his hand. "If it's the same Mrs. Murphy who is Floria's neighbor, she's writing a new will at least twice a year and pitching her many nephews one against the other with the promise of inheriting. One of them is the High School Principal. Also they think she has a pile of money, when the only thing of value she has, is her old Arts and Crafts house, if it was in truth designed by Frank Lloyd Wright's disciple, I forgot his name. But enough about this. I have a more lucrative project for you."

"You strangled Wilma Jenkins and need a defense attorney," Michael anticipated with a fighting sparkle in his eyes.

"No. No. It's much better than that. I want you to evict the Country Club from the premises," Charlie announced in a calm voice.

Michael dropped the doggy biscuit with which he

was teasing Scruffy. "Say this again! You want me to do what?"

"The Country Club and their Golfing business are renting the golf course and the main building from a company called CC Development. The Country Club has to maintain the Golf Course, the grounds, the whole property, which they did, but in the last three years they forgot to pay the rent. The letters sent to them asking for the overdue rent money went unanswered. I have here the rental agreement and copies of the certified letters. The company wants the Club evicted. They have other plans for the property. Can you do that?"

Michael studied the papers, looked at Charlie and said, "What else can the company do with a golf course?"

"Is this your only question? Rest assured it will still be a golf course, accessible to all who are willing to pay a small fee for using it, enough to cover the maintenance. You realize that this is not going to endear you to the high and mighty in town. Again you might loose business."

"On the contrary, being a feared adversary makes one a desired attorney." Michael rubbed his hands. "Of course I'll do it Charlie. I can hardly wait. You provided me with more excitement that I dared hope for. Who knew life in Hunters Crossing could be so exciting?"

"Yeah! Who knew? Come on, Scruffy! We're leaving."

CHAPTER 18

Charlie stopped near Starbucks to attach the leash to Scruffy's collar. He heard a voice calling him, "Coach Callahan! Charlie!" Being ignored lately by most of his so-called friends, Charlie turned surprised. Officer Tramontana in uniform was smiling friendly. "How are you Coach? I haven't seen you in a while. The kids are missing you and are …disoriented without your guidance."

"Well, I…" What could Charlie say? That he was not only missing his team, but also feeling like he had abandoned them. Not willingly abandoned, but the responsibility for the team's success was his. "I'll fix it and come back. Soon," he promised.

"I hope so. Otherwise the kids will riot and where will I be. My son is bugging me all the time, asking me when you'll come back."

"Your son?" Charlie didn't remember any Tramontana on the team.

"Ryan Walker. He doesn't have my last name. A

long story, for another time."

"Walker... Sure. Talented running back."

"He'll be proud you said so. Thank you for encouraging him to apply to go to college on a football scholarship. He'd been through so much. He didn't have confidence in himself at all. You helped him a lot." The officer smiled. "Now I have to run." He raised two fingers to his cap and turned to go. Then changed his mind and stopped. "Tell you what. Some friends of mine, we meet at Lou's Tavern every week. Tonight at 7-ish. We play some pool, joke, drink a beer, watch sports. If you're hungry, Lou has some burgers to die for. If you'd like to come you'd be most welcome among us, you Hall of Fame hero. That lawyer fellow accepted very enthusiastically. He said he'll be there."

"You know Michael Fraser?" Charlie asked surprised.

"Sure I do. First, because I know everybody who lives in Hunters Crossing and second, because he came to talk to me about the upcoming meeting in court, because I was there right after the confrontation. I can tell you, lawyer Weinstein didn't talk to me. Michael Fraser is a great guy…. Now I have to go. See you tonight if you decide to come."

Then he was gone. "Eh, Scruffy what do you say? You'll have to wait for me in the car, at least in the beginning. It's not too cold and I'll be back with a burger for you. I know you like Kibbles'n Bits, but once in a while it's good to indulge in a burger," Charlie said opening the door to his truck. "I forgot to correct him. I was not a Hall of Famer. I was proposed a few times, but didn't have enough votes."

Lou's Tavern was in a not so affluent part of town. Smaller houses, some run-down. The tavern itself was about the same as Charlie remembered it from his younger days. The sign had some missing lights. The interior was dark without much light. There was loud country music, and television sets in all corners.

Charlie approached the bar and took a seat. A young girl with a come-on smile asked him what he wanted to drink, only to be pushed aside gently. Lou himself set a foaming beer in front of him. "Hello Charlie! I haven't seen you for a long time," he said in his raspy voice.

"Then you have a very good memory, Lou, if you remember me." Charlie raised the glass and savored the unique taste of Lou's beer. He used to brew it himself.

"Memory has nothing to do with it. This dratted town is so small we all know each other's business. Especially yours. We are waiting to see what comes next. Willing or not, you are a celebrity in this town."

Was this a good thing or was Lou mocking him? Charlie was not sure. "Tell me, have you seen Officer Tramontana?" he asked in order to change the subject of his recently acquired celebrity.

"Oscar is in the back playing pool," Lou said, inclining his head in that direction.

Charlie grabbed his beer and marched through the curtain that separated the two rooms. A bunch of guys dressed in jeans and flannel shirts were gathered around the pool table, cheering on Oscar Tramontana who was trying to hit the right ball at the right angle. Oops!

Missed. The guys cheered nevertheless.

"Hey fellow!" one of them said raising his beer. "Why don't you try? Let's see what you can do?"

At first, Charlie thought they were talking about him and he knew himself. At the amateur level, he was unbeatable in any sport, pool and bowling included. No reason showing off here.

Two guys stepped aside and Michael Fraser, dressed in an impeccable charcoal grey suit, white shirt and blue tie approached the table, offering them a timid smile. Drat the man! He stood out like a peacock in a yard full of chickens. He took the cue and rubbed it for a long time, increasing the tension around the table. Then he pushed his glasses up on his nose, moved this way and that way to study the angles and deciding how to strike. One could hear moans of impatience. Then he moved the cue so fast, like a cobra striking its prey. The ball was sunk in the corner. Again and again. The men were starting to clap and cheer him on. Until there was no ball on the table. Then he straightened, pushed his glasses up again, and the shy smile was back on his face.

"Oh man! I can't believe he's so good," someone said.

"Michael, you did well!" Tramontana said, patting him on the back. "Maybe you want to take off your jacket to be more comfortable. Charlie, you know Ken, from Ken's Garage and Towing."

Of course Charlie knew Ken. Every time Lorena wrecked or scratched the BMW, they needed Ken's services. Now that Billy Bob started driving the SUV, they'd need him even more.

"And this is Tony Mendoza, our fire chief," Tramontana continued. They shook hands. Charlie didn't know Mendoza personally, no fire yet at his house, but with the recent going-ons in the kitchen and intense activity, they might. Tony Mendoza was as tall as Tramontana, and strongly built, with a permanent frown on his face.

"And there is his brother," Tramontana presented again. "Hey, Lyle!"

Farther away, a man surrounded by four or five females was throwing darts, eliciting Oohs and Ahs and sighs with every throw. Most of the darts were gathered in the bulls-eye. He was very good. He was also very handsome, tall as his brother, not as wide, but with the strength of an athlete. His face had perfect masculine features, from his square jaw and sensual mouth to his soulful dark eyes with long lashes. The women liked what they saw.

Lyle Mendoza raised his hand in salute, but didn't bother coming closer.

CHAPTER 19

Lorena stepped into the kitchen and collapsed in a chair at the table. Billy Bob, who

had decided the kids needed more nutritional food than pizza, was experimenting a couscous with mushroom and herbs recipe. It sounded rather bland, but the aroma coming from his pot was very tempting. The day before, he had cooked an eggplant casserole that had made them all ask for seconds. Eggplant was a vegetable Lorena didn't know how to cook and therefore avoided it.

"Hey Princess, did something upset you today? Made you sad?" Billy Bob said placing a tea mug in front of her and a plate with little quiches which they were preparing for an upcoming catering event. "I have some good news."

Any day Lorena would have welcomed good news. Today however, her bad news was so overwhelming that she felt the need to cry. "Oh Billy Bob, what am I going to do? Today, the Ladies Circle of

Quilting and Gardening are meeting at the Country Club and my friend Violet told me that Wilma Jenkins will ask me to be excluded from the Club as not worthy to be a member."

Billy Bob turned off the heat under the couscous and came to sit at the table. "Why would you be considered unworthy? Unless you told them you don't like sewing anything and that means quilts too and that gardening means telling Thomas to bring the herbs containers closer to the house and to plant more tulip bulbs up front. By the way is this Ladies Circle inspired after the Knights of the Round Table?"

Lorena smiled through her tears. "Don't make me laugh, Billy Bob. They think I'm not good enough for the club as the wife of a man accused of assaulting a lady and because I grew up in a trailer park. Violet thinks I should not come to avoid being humiliated."

"Listen to me. First, you are already a member of the Club, pardon Circle, and considered worthy. You did nothing of which to be ashamed and what your husband did or didn't do is not the issue here. Violet might be your best friend, but she gave you lousy advice. You go out there head high and dare them to tell you to your face that you are not worthy."

On second thought, Billy Bob was right. She should go. "Oh, I could strangle Charlie for creating this situation," she cried in frustration.

"Be honest, you don't know what happened. He might have been provoked..." Billy Bob said gently.

"Yes, maybe," she conceded. "All right, I'm going."

"Good girl! And don't forget that if push comes to shove, you don't care about their stupid Circle."

"I care about what it represents. What will I do otherwise?"

He shrugged. "Make your own Circle. I bet ladies will come in flocks to be part of it."

She laughed and went to dress. Not in the boring beige suit this time. She chose the blue dress and assorted accessories and Lorena was ready for the meeting. Before leaving she paused in the kitchen door. "Thank you, Billy Bob..... For being here when I needed you."

The drive to the Country Club calmed her instead of increasing her anxiety. She replayed in her mind what Billy Bob had said and smiled.

She marched right in and took her place near Violet. Her friend looked surprised to see her and pulled her chair farther apart. "Good afternoon, ladies," Lorena said, like her mama taught her to be polite all the time even if they lived in a trailer park. She smiled and looked around her. Some were as surprised to see her as Violet. Some smiled back in response. Bridget, Wilma's friend emitted a nervous giggle, her hand covering her mouth and Molly Malone nodded her head in acknowledgement.

"Well, we thought you wouldn't show your face today, Mrs. Callahan," Wilma said in an acerbic tone.

Ah, the play was about to begin. Lorena straightened her spine and smiled. "Then you were wrong, Wilma, as usual. But why did you think I would not come?"

Wilma puffed. "The wife of a man who assaulted..."

Lorena interrupted her. "My husband is not here and what he does is not a subject up for discussion in this meeting." That took a bit of the wind from her sails. But not for long.

"Ladies," Wilma started again, twitching her long nose, "as we talked before, we have among us a person who is not worthy, considering her relatives, past and present,…I understand there is now a bastard daughter come to live with them."

"Bastard daughter," Lorena exploded, "where and when do you think you live, Wilma? Charles Dickens' times? Amanda is a lawyer in Washington DC. And don't you dare touch my family…"

"You see ladies, in the end her deplorable manners show. I don't know who introduced you into our Circle, because Violet said it was not her."

"Theresa Hunter herself persuaded me to join the Circle, although I told her I never quilted in my life and gardening was not my number one passion. She persisted though."

This gave Wilma a pause. Not long after, she

recovered her aplomb. "Nevertheless, I think that as she admitted not sharing our passion for finer things in life and no wonder that, considering where she was raised, she should be excluded…"

"No." The word was said in a quiet, but firm voice that stopped Wilma's speech with the power of a bullet. It was Molly Malone. "No, not because Theresa Hunter considered her good enough or because she didn't do anything at all to warrant this drastic exclusion. No, because this is so arbitrary and unfair that it means it can happen to anyone of us." She looked around them. "I love quilting and growing prize roses is my passion, but I'll stop coming here if this Circle is not anymore what it was at the beginning, a Circle of friends."

Lorena felt her eyes mist with tears. "That was so nice of you to say, Molly. I hope we are a Circle of friends." She turned to Violet. "I wanted to ask you about little Toby's party if a race cars themed party, as he likes race cars, would be agreeable."

Her friend didn't meet her eyes. "About that I wanted to tell you that Victor said we'll keep it simple and we'll not need your help any more."

Lorena was stunned. "Why? Billy Bob has arranged to bring real trophies won by his friend…"

"Ah, the famous or infamous should I say, father-in-law. The one whose financial schemes caused so many people to lose their money," Wilma cackled with glee. "Now he is a party organizer. People should count their silver."

Narrowing her eyes, Lorena turned. "Careful Wilma, malicious slander is a very good reason for a lawsuit and if I lose business I can ask for monetary compensation. Unlike you, I have plenty of witnesses." She shook her head. "Ladies, this Circle is not anymore what Theresa Hunter envisioned. Molly is right. Instead of helping the town prosper and instead of supporting each other, it has deteriorated into a platform for patronizing and bullying each other and spreading malicious rumors. Therefore, I resign my membership. Have a very good day all." She went out head high as she had come.

At home, she collapsed in her chair at the kitchen table.

"Well, I hope you didn't let them exclude you," Billy Bob asked hovering behind her with tea, more tea and cookies.

"No, I sure didn't," Lorena said, sipping the strong, fragrant tea. "I did much, much better. I resigned." Billy Bob sat in the next chair abruptly, the teapot swaying in his hand. "Hey, watch out with that teapot. It's real Wedgewood porcelain."

"But why?" he asked.

Lorena considered the question. "Because I wanted. For the first time I did what I wanted."

"But you said you wanted to be part of this Circle."

"It's complicated. The truth is I don't want to be a member, not to mention that since the catering business started I don't have time. But not being part of the Ladies Circle is … like a social suicide. Resigning was satisfying, but I'm not sure it was smart. Not even for business." Billy Bob smiled his Cheshire cat smile.

"What? Do you know something I don't?"

"Lorena, I can tell you that Charlie has more weight in this town than you think. He is like those sleeping giants who once awake should be feared."

Lorena waved her hand. "Charlie has his own problems. If the Judge decides that there is cause and he goes to trial, his life will be quite complicated. The Judge plays golf with the Mayor. He is fair, but in the end we are all human. Besides I wanted to succeed just this once on my own."

"And you will. Remember the good news I was about to tell you. Well, our webpage was very successful. Guess what? A couple from Cincinnati has a wedding in a little more than three weeks and the bride fired the catering firm for whatever reason. Browsing the web she saw our page and fell in love with our cake remember?...The one with the doves. So, she called us to ask if we're willing to take over the catering."

"Wow" Lorena was dazed. To cater a big affair such as a wedding in a city like Cincinnati was... big. It represented the peak for a catering business.

"Well, what do you say?" Billy Bob asked.

"What can I say? It seems we're in business, partner."

CHAPTER 20

Ding, dong!

"God, I hate the bell ringing," Lorena muttered while placing rows of sugar rosebuds on a platter to dry.

Ding, dong!

"I hope they are the boys from the Latter-day Saints Church."

Billy Bob looked at her surprised. "Why is that? You intend to convert to the Mormons?"

Lorena laughed. "Of course not. I'd kill all the other wives Charlie might have."

"You love him that much?"

"I don't know about love. I'm possessive I guess."

Ding, dong!

"I'll answer," Amanda shouted coming down the stairs. She slipped on the marble floor at the entrance and almost twisted her ankle. "This had better be good," she muttered opening the door.

And it was. Good, incredible, stupendous. The

most handsome man she had seen in her life. And she'd seen a lot of them. In Washington DC, men dressed in Armani suits were at every corner and most of them were handsome. She was not a dreamy-eyed girl. But on the front porch, stood an amazing example of masculine splendor. Pardon her for thinking in terms of romance novels, but how else could she describe this perfection. Tall, dark, and handsome would be clichéd, lacking originality. He was all that and more, athletic, muscular, without being beefy, long legs in dark jeans, nice pecs, revealed by the tight t-shirt he wore. He carried his jacket in one hand. Amanda raised her eyes. A square jaw, clean shaved, - she hated the stubble some men sported thinking they were sexy - dark hair cut short, sensual lips curved in a half smile revealing white, bright teeth. Were those dimples? She thought his eyes were black, but looking closely she saw they were midnight blue.

"Will I do?" he asked in a low voice that sent tingles down her spine.

Oh dear, he caught her not only staring at him, but gawking. "I…I…," she babbled.

His smile deepened. "For a lawyer you are surprisingly slow of speech, Amanda."

"Do you know me?" she asked. For she was certain she'd never seen him in her life. He was that memorable.

"Of course. Charlie told us a lot about you. He's very proud of you."

"Oh I see. You came to see Charlie. He's in the garage working on his bike, although why? I don't know. I understand he never went for a ride," Amanda said.

The dimples appeared again. "Yes, I wanted to see him, but I also wanted to invite you to have dinner with me," he said, raising his hand and offering her one, most perfect rose. A peach colored old rose with a fragrance that perfumed the air. "My name is Lyle, Lyle Mendoza."

"This is beautiful," she exclaimed burying her nose in the soft petals.

"Does this mean you accept? Saturday at 7."

Amanda looked at him open-mouthed. "Wait a minute. Dinner? As in a date?"

"Yes," he confirmed. "Dinner date. Saturday at 7. Yes."

"But you don't know me, even if you heard about me. And I don't know you."

"All these are good reasons to get to know each other. What's wrong with that?"

"B…Because I'm not so impulsive…" she stuttered.

"Look, people meet and date strangers all the time in the era of internet dating and online matchmaking. No time to waste. If you are afraid of me being a stranger, then Charlie and a few other pillars of this community can vouch for me."

"Did Charlie put you up to this? Inviting his pathetic daughter out to dinner?"

Now he looked affronted. "I am too old to do anybody's bidding and you are not pathetic. And Charlie, he might not be pleased with this. He'll vouch I'm safe, not a dangerous lunatic, but I'm not so sure he considers me good enough to date his precious daughter. No matter. I'm going now to talk to him. So will you Miss

Amanda do me the honor to have dinner with me?"

"Yes, yes I will."

"Saturday at 7 I'll come and pick you up." His wonderful smile appeared again and he left whistling.

Amanda sighed, closed the door, and waltzed into the kitchen.

"You will not believe what happened to me," she announced, sliding on one of the chairs.

Billy Bob ceased stirring in the pan and turned around. "Jeesh, you converted to them Mormons?"

"What? No, no. Something more incredible. I'll tell you all when Charlie comes in and we have dinner."

Later that evening, they all gathered around the kitchen table and Lorena set her famous vegetarian risotto on the table and Billy Bob presented them with piping hot meatballs and a fresh Caesar Salad to be eaten with the risotto. Lorena had read online that Italians eat their salad together with the main course, not before. Strange habits.

Charlie was morose. Drew was ebullient and full

of energy. A writer of children stories had seen his drawings and invited him to submit some samples to be considered as illustrations for the book. Lorena was absent-minded thinking about the wedding she had to plan. The photographer and the flowers were taken care of, and the dresses too. The food menu could use some changes. Three weeks was not enough for all that remained to be done. Scruffy knew he was not allowed in the kitchen and usually he was happy with his doggy food, but he was intrigued by the smell of the meatballs. He hid under Drew's chair and waited.

Billy Bob was watching Amanda who was in a dream-like state. "Now tell us Amanda who had been at the door," he asked.

Charlie looked up from his plate. "Yes Amanda, why don't you tell us?" he asked too.

Amanda looked from one to the other, and then shrugged, "A very handsome man asked me out on a date. And I said 'yes'."

"Wait a minute!" Lorena said, "Who do you know here in Hunters Crossing?"

"He is a very good friend of Charlie. His name is Lyle Mendoza." Amanda turned to Charlie. "I suppose he didn't lie. You do know him and it is safe for me to spend the evening in his company."

After a brief hesitation, Charlie nodded, "Yes."

Amanda wanted to inquire further, when Lorena exclaimed loudly, "Oh my God, not Lyle, brother to Tony Mendoza!"

"Why not, what's wrong with him?" Amanda asked.

"The Mendoza brothers grew up in a trailer park, dirt poor. Hellions, both of them. No mother and an alcoholic father. He beat them when he was drunk. Tony hung out with the firefighters ever since he was a little boy. I heard he's the fire chief now."

"And Lyle?"

Lorena looked horrified. "Oh Amanda, Lyle is the Trashman."

"What Lorena wants to say," Charlie interrupted, "is that after years of enduring abuse from his father, Lyle worked every job he could get, delivering newspapers, helping people move, working for the waste pick-up company. He put away all the money, invested it, and became partner in the waste company. When the previous owner died he left the entire company to Lyle. He put himself through college. Right now he is a successful businessman, owning the local trash pick-up company, a moving and moving supplies company, and a very large place with rental storage spaces. At least that's all I know. He's a shrewd businessman, hard working and yes! he's known in a derogatory way as the Trashman, because when he has shortage of personnel, he is not too proud to drive one of his trucks and take a pick-up route himself."

"That's remarkable! Good for him!" Amanda exclaimed.

"You can't be serious!?" Lorena admonished her. "I mean, have fun with him, but don't get too close. Think about it. If he is treated as Trashman here in Hunters Crossing, how acceptable do you think he will be in the highly snobbish political society in Washington DC?"

"No, this is not an impediment. On the contrary. I could make it very appealing. Self-made man, hard working. That is if he wants to run for office," Amanda said with enthusiasm. "This is what I am; a political advisor and strategist. For now however, we are only going to a dinner date. That's all. Might be no chemistry at all." She turned again to Charlie. "Now, you tell me what are your reservations. I am getting mixed signals from you. You admire him, but you...don't want me to go out with him. Why?"

Charlie pushed away his empty plate on the table. "Amanda, you know I love you, or maybe you don't. I do want the best for you. Lyle is a remarkable man as you said, but he is thirty-eight years old, eleven years older than you and..." He raised his hand when Amanda wanted to protest. "...he is always surrounded by females. He is a ladies' man and I don't want to see you hurt."

"Is he promiscuous? Makes promises he doesn't keep?"

"No, no. He is an honorable man, but he can't

help it, I suppose. Ladies are attracted to him, like bees to honey, wherever he goes."

Amanda gathered some empty plates and placed them in the sink. "Don't worry people, I will go on this date, nothing serious, and we'll see what happens." She started to load the dishwasher and then she turned back. "What am I going to do? I have nothing to wear."

CHAPTER 21

It was a cold, rainy day in November. The Courthouse was packed with people, some seating on the benches, others standing up; all waiting for the Honorable Judge Arthur J Rollins to come in and start the day's scheduled events. One would think a notorious criminal trial was about to start, when in fact there was no trial. The Judge was supposed to decide if this complaint should go in front of a jury as a trial or not.

Charlie looked around him and saw Floria, seating right behind him, whispering 'Good luck'. She had to come very early to get a seat in the first public row. Behind her, Amanda and Drew were smiling and waving encouragingly and near Amanda, Lyle Mendoza. In the back, some of the gang from Lou's Tavern was present, including Lyle's brother Tony, Ken, the mechanic, and a few others. You'd think there was no business going on in town. No cars to fix at Ken's garage or fire to extinguish somewhere. Was that Lou himself, hiding behind the fire chief? A day of wonders when the

Tavern was closed during the day.

It seemed the pets were unusually healthy today, so Leonard Wiseman, the veterinarian was smiling at him from the right side of the room with a beautiful young woman on his arm. Young enough to be his daughter. Then Charlie remembered that Leo had a grown-up daughter. Leo was talking to an older man, a retired banker also from the golf playing people. There were a lot of other people from the Country Club, including President Mahoney, looking very gloomy. No wonder. Charlie knew that the day before, he had been given the eviction papers for the Club from the premises. Mahoney wrote a protest to the Judge, but 'good luck with that'. The law was clear. The Club had not paid the rent for three years; the owner had the right to evict.

A noisy group at the back of the room, his high school football team, had come to support their favorite Coach. Charlie wondered if Judge Rollins would be able to keep the room quiet with such a boisterous group present.

There were so many people that Charlie didn't

know who was on his side and who had come to see his downfall. There was a young investor banker from Cincinnati who had recently bought a luxurious condo in the new development overlooking Silver Lake. He was very active in the Country Club (he was somebody's nephew) and golfing was his passion, that was why he had moved to Hunters Crossing, he had confessed. He waved at Charlie and gave him a thumb up in support.

Two people were notably absent from the room. One of them was the Mayor himself. As his wife was the complainer, the Mayor thought his presence might be construed as influencing the justice and God forbid that anybody would think that. But of course he could be in the back rooms of the courthouse talking to the Judge. The other person absent was Lorena. Even Billy Bob squeezed himself on the bench near Drew and gave Charlie a tentative smile and a salute. Was Lorena still mad at him or only busy with her catering business? Charlie sighed. No point being negative. Michael, seated beside him, looking very dashing in his elegant suit, winked at him, as if saying, 'Piece of cake. Don't worry.'

On the other side of the aisle, Wilma Jenkins and her lawyer, Jacob Weinstein were whispering, heads bent together, not that anyone could hear what they said in the all-around noise.

The court clerk came in and said, "All rise for the Honorable Judge Arthur J Rollins."

The Judge, a middle aged-man with snow white hair and gold rimmed glasses, raised an eyebrow when he saw the room overpacked with people. "So much interest in our activities I haven't seen since five years ago when we caught Aaron Dunn trying to rob the bank. At the trial he claimed he was Jesse James reincarnated and couldn't help history repeating."

The Judge shuffled the papers on his desk. "Now, Mrs. Wilma Jenkins is accusing Mr. Charles Callahan of insulting and assaulting her. Let's hear her story. Mr. Weinstein you start."

Jacob Weinstein rose slowly from his seat. "Your Honor, my client was grievously injured. First, she was insulted and then physically assaulted, hit and pushed by the accused. And … " he paused to create a dramatic effect. "… He didn't deny it. Mr. Callahan admitted in front of a police officer that he did this. " He turned to Charlie. "I call Mrs. Wilma Jenkins to stand for questioning."

The Mayor's wife stood up and went to the witness box.

The lawyer approached her. "Mrs. Jenkins, is it true that Mr. Callahan called you…" He looked at the paper he had in his hand. "quote, 'an ugly biddy'?"

Wilma nodded. "An ugly, old biddy. Yes."

There were hoots of laughter in the room. Even some whistles.

"Quiet, quiet in the court," the judge demanded. "Continue Mr. Weinstein."

The lawyer nodded. "Is it true that Mr. Callahan hit your arm and pushed you?"

Michael jumped. "Objection, Your Honor. He is leading the witness."

The judge considered this. "Overruled. You, Mr. Fraser, you will have the opportunity to tell your story more in detail when your turn comes. I like things in order. Answer the question Mrs. Jenkins."

"Yes, that's what he did. He assaulted me," Wilma said.

The lawyer nodded satisfied. "And did he confirm this to the police officer?"

Wilma looked at Charlie. "He admitted to all this and the police officer wrote all this down in his reportbook. Too bad he didn't arrest him. He should have."

There were murmurs in the room and Weinstein perused the audience satisfied. "You see your Honor, the accused admitted to the facts. We don't need anybody else to attest to this, as there were no other people present, except Mrs. Jenkins' friend who was distracted when all this happened."

"All right Mr. Weinstein," the Judge said. "Mr. Fraser do you have any questions for this witness?"

Michael stood up and said, "No questions for now. We reserve the right to call back Mrs. Jenkins latter."

Wilma went back to her place and for the first

time since the afternoon of the game, Charlie thought Lorena was right, and that he might loose. Michael was smiling as if they were not a step away from disaster.

"Mr. Weinstein, do you have any other witnesses," asked the Judge.

"No other witnesses your Honor"

"Mr. Fraser. Your argument," the Judge invited.

Michael stood up again, pushed his glasses up on his nose, and turned slightly to face the Judge and also partly the room. "That afternoon everybody was sad because our high school football team had lost the game with their rivals from Clarksville…"

"Objection, Your Honor. This is irrelevant. It has nothing to do with the assault," Weinstein objected.

The judge looked from one lawyer to the other. "Maybe yes, maybe not. But we all deserve to know what happened in detail. Overruled. Go on Mr. Fraser."

"The loss affected everybody and the parents, friends and relatives didn't linger to talk as usual. Coach Callahan was looking for a friend, he wanted to talk to, and left the team's bench and went to the bleachers to look for him. But the friend had left. The stadium was almost empty, when he heard a voice speaking behind him," Michael paused. "Now I call Mrs. Jenkins to the stand."

The judge nodded and Wilma Jenkins, dressed all in funereal black took the seat again.

Michael approached her. "Mrs. Jenkins, when you saw Coach Callahan, did you say to your friend – quote, 'Drew Callahan was a disaster. We have better players, but he is kept on the field because of who his father is.' Did you say this?"

As rehearsed before with her lawyer, Wilma said, "I don't remember." Then sensing victory was close, she added, "But it's true. Drew Callahan is a disaster that day, and there are others more talented…," she said warming up to the subject. "My own son, Sammy, is so much better and he was rejected from the team by Coach Callahan only to promote his own inept son."

Michael smiled at her and in a soft, gentle voice he continued his questioning, "And then Coach said – quote, 'You don't know what you're talking about.'

Correct?"

Wilma nodded. "That's right. That's what he said."

"Then you added – quote, 'Drew Callahan is sissy and gay. He shouldn't be part of the team. He's a disgrace.' Correct?"

There were waves of murmurs and exclamations from the room, but Michael was focused on Wilma, coaxing her gently to talk to him, like in a restaurant where two make conversation regardless of the surrounding noise.

Wilma paused considering, and then shrugged. "Yes. That is correct. And all of it is true. It's a shame to have a gay person among our boys."

Charlie winced. Maybe Michael knew what he was doing, but thinking of the ordeal Drew was going through, he regretted causing all this scandal for his son. If he could take it back he would.

Meanwhile, Michael beamed at Wilma. "Thank you, Mrs. Jenkins. If I'll need your help further, I'll call you back. You can step down." He turned to the Judge.

"We would like to call Officer Oscar Tramontana."

The Officer came down the aisle to the witness stand.

Michael approached him. "I understand that you were at the stadium when all this happened."

"Yes. I was in charge of the security during the game and when the stadium emptied I was looking for lost objects. You'd be surprised how many there are, jackets, backpacks, phones, sunglasses and so on. Usually I gather them and take them to the Janitor's room. The kids know to look for them there. At some point a car started honking in the parking lot and I looked there, worried some prankster might do something. Then I heard a female voice crying for help, so I went back to see what happened."

"And what did you see?" Michael asked.

The officer made an hmm…hmm! sound and answered. "I saw Coach Callahan, drenched in a brown liquid, soda I suppose, with bits of ice clinging to his t-shirt and liquid dripping from his hair and eyebrows. Near him, a hysterical woman, Mrs. Jenkins…"

"Objection!" cried attorney Weinstein.

"Pardon me, sir," the officer replied. "But she was hysterical, shouting, 'Arrest him, arrest him.' "

"Then what did you do?" Michael asked.

"Before arresting anyone I have to investigate. After the game, they exchanged heated words and insults and Mrs. Jenkins threw her extra large size drink in Coach's face and as a reflexive gesture, he pushed her hand away. The empty cup fell to the ground. I saw no reason for arrest. I told them both to cool down and go home."

"Thank you, Officer," Michael said going back near Charlie.

Jacob Weinstein rose and approached the officer.

"Officer Tramontana, are you a friend of Charlie Callahan?"

The officer nodded. "I am, Yes. I hope I am." And he smiled at Charlie.

Weinstein continued in his oily voice. "And is it possible that this friendship might have influenced your actions and now your memory?"

Tramontana looked at him. "No, it is not possible. I am an officer of the law and we have procedures to follow. I investigated, wrote everything in my notebook, both Mrs. Jenkins and Coach agreed on every word I wrote. Mrs. Jenkins friend corroborated, at least the part to which she had been present. Then I wrote the official police report, with all the details. Well except the part where Mrs. Jenkins threatened to have me fired for not arresting the Coach. And then she started sprouting all sort of nonsense like 'Do I know who she is? A descendant of Thomas Jefferson, that's who she is'. I assumed she talked in a figurative sense. After all, we all could claim to descend from the founding fathers."

"Quiet!" demanded the Judge, when the audience started laughing. He turned to Michael. "Are you done, Mr. Fraser?"

"One last witness, your Honor. We are calling Tom Gorman."

One of the students from the back approached the stand. Michael came in front of him. "Mr. Gorman, could you tell us who you are and how long have you known

Coach Callahan?"

"My name is Tom Gorman and I'm a senior in high school and I am a member of the football team. I've known personally Coach Callahan for almost four years."

Michael inclined his head. "Very well. In all these years when you had weekly training and other occasions, did you hear him swearing at students, insulting, being aggressive in any way, pushing or hitting anyone, losing his temper?"

Tom Gorman shook his head. "No sir, never. Football is a physically aggressive game. Pushing, even swearing and other stuff are part of the game. Yet, even when showing us how to play, Coach is careful that nobody get hurt. I have never seen him losing his temper, ever. All my teammates can confirm this. But, if someone talked about me like that woman did about Drew, my father would be real mad and violent. And I'd expect no less, 'cause if my father won't defend me, who will?"

"Thank you, Mr. Gorman. You may go," Michael said softly.

The Judge took his glasses off, rubbed his eyes and said, "All right. Closing arguments. Mr. Weinstein."

The lawyer rose again. His voice was really pompous and condescending, Charlie thought.

"We heard here all sorts of depositions. How it was a lost game and people were agitated. Coach Callahan never looses his temper, but in this case he did." Weinstein approached Charlie's bench and continued increasing the tone. "And all arguments aside, he did insult Mrs. Jenkins and pushed her. This is assault. And this is what he admitted. He…" Weinstein was close to Charlie now and pointed his finger at him accusatory. "He is…" In that moment, cool as you pleased, Michael, seated next to Charlie, rose and grabbed the glass of water in front of him and threw it in the face of the astonished attorney. Weinstein, shocked, pushed Michael back down on the bench.

"Mr. Fraser!" cried the Judge.

"Yes, your Honor," Michael replied, all a picture of innocence. "What?! It's not like I assaulted him, did I? It was only water during a heated argument. Or did he assault me? After all he pushed me almost under the table…Hmm! You think I should sue him perhaps?"

The Court exploded with noise, arguments and laughter.

"Quiet!" shouted the Judge, but not many people could hear him. After a while, when people quieted down, the Judge said shaking his finger at Michael, "I could forbid you to plead in my Court in the future. Let me make it clear to you. I will not have my Court transformed in a Circus. Do we understand each other?"

"Yes, sir. But you know what the French say, "A la guerre comme a la guerre! This is what happens in a war."

"No war, no French. Not in my Court." But the corner of his mouth was twitching with laughter. "Case dismissed," he concluded, banging his gavel.

CHAPTER 22

There were hands shaking and back slapping, and congratulations. And applauses and laughter all around him. And the football team surrounding him like puppies, eager to know when he'd be back. And the image of Floria jumping up and down like she were seventeen again, joy in her eyes. And Amanda and Drew high-five-ing, and Billy Bob giving him a jaunty salute, this time with a real smile before disappearing in the sea of people.

Charlie turned to Michael and shook hands. "You said you were good when in truth, you are brilliant. Thank you, Michael."

He felt a hand gripping his arm. He turned. "Victor!"

Victor gave him a hesitant half smile. "I'm glad all this is over. I'm very glad."

"Yes, so am I," Charlie said, gently disengaging his arm from Victor's hold.

"I wanted to say that I am very sorry for all that

162

happened. I wish I could have acted in a different way, but I couldn't."

"Sure you could, we all have choices."

"I couldn't…You don't understand…," Victor wanted to explain but looked at all the people around them. "Never mind. Look, maybe I'll see you on the golf course sometime."

"Yeah, maybe…sometime," Charlie echoed. Victor was gone and Charlie wondered if this was meant to be Victor's version of an excuse. He was sorry to see a long friendship end like this. It was not that he was resentful. But he could not be friends with someone he didn't trust.

It was a long time before Charlie finished talking with all the well-wishers and made his way to his car. All he wanted was to go home and sleep until the next day. He drove to Floria instead.

She opened the door and hugged him. "Charlie, how did you know I wanted to see you? I thought today for sure you'll be busy."

"Busy doing what?"

"Busy celebrating, enjoying life."

Charlie laughed, following her into the kitchen. "That's what I'm doing. With you. How could I not, Flori? You have been my friend, my support."

She turned to him and hugged him again. "Oh Charlie, I'm so glad I found you again." She raised her eyes and they were moist with tears. "You are so dear to me."

Charlie realized it was true. He felt a tremendous love for this older version of his young girlfriend. Sometimes, in a smile or in a spontaneous gesture, like clapping her hands in delight, he could see the young Floria. However, he knew without a doubt that he adored the older version as well, for her unfailing support and loyalty, for her gentle ways of caring for him, and for giving him confidence and good advice. In return, he wanted to take her in his arms and soothe her tears and chase her worries away.

"Charlie, I wanted to tell you that I sold the house."

"This house?" Charlie asked dumbfounded. He

knew she wanted to sell her mother's house, but it was too soon, way too soon. He wanted to spend more time with her. What would she do now?"

She laughed through her tears. "Yes, this house. When I came to settle my mothers' estate I thought two weeks would be enough. It's been four months. I had a buyer who offered me a little more than half the market value of the house. The market value takes in consideration the size of the house and the location, not the condition which in this case is pretty bad. This house needs a lot of repairs. So I accepted the offer."

"You could live at…"

She put a finger on his lips to stop him. "I'm leaving tomorrow. Back home to California."

"Oh Flori, what will I do? I can't live without you."

"Yes, you can Charlie. But I want you to know that I value our friendship very much and I hope we'll keep in touch. E-mails, text messages, phone calls. You see, in California I have friends, neighbors, and my daughter, but it's very important for me to know that there is someone like you who cares, who loves me unconditionally, just because I exist in this world. You can rely on my support always. Our young, passionate love changed or evolved into a very precious feeling. Because let's be honest we don't have that sexual chemistry we had at seventeen, but there is a stronger, more meaningful love between us." Floria said with tears of sadness mixed with a small smile of hope and encouragement.

Charlie realized how insightful Floria was. It was true. There was no sexual attraction between them, but it was love nevertheless and tenderness and the desire to take her in his arms and never let her go. He needed her so much. She was a vital part of his life. How could he let her go?

"Promise me we'll keep in touch," Floria said again.

"Of course. I promise."

"And I promise I'll come back to see you. Soon. Until then, let's say not 'Good bye', which has a finality to it, but 'Au revoir' - I'll be seeing you again. "

"I'll take you to the airport in Cincinnati."

"No Charlie. I couldn't bear to part at the airport. Go now." She kissed him softly on the lips.

That was it. Without looking back, he left her house.

CHAPTER 23

At home, tantalizing aromas were coming from the kitchen, a sign that something good was cooking there. These days something good was always cooking in his kitchen, only not for him, Charlie thought, leaning against the door frame. Lorena was stirring the pots on the stovetop. She was still a very beautiful woman, looking at least ten years younger. She had that delicate, slim figure, a fragile blond, blue-eyed beauty that ignited admiration and protective feelings in men, making them want to prove strong and macho. Of course, Lorena was not fragile. She had always been very tough. She had to be tough in order to survive.

She had been a great mother. Their two boys adored her. She kept a balance between discipline and indulgence, instilling in them a sense of responsibility to have worthy goals in life and work hard to achieve them.

Charlie continued to watch her and Lorena raised a hand to a falling strand of hair and placed it back in the scrunchie that kept her hair up. It was such a soft, feminine gesture. A beautiful woman and a good wife. He was a lucky dog, Charlie thought. Sex between them had always been very satisfying. Lorena was an eager, imaginative partner. Even now, after twenty years of marriage, when she walked in their bedroom in her underwear, Charlie felt his desire for her rising. Not many men could claim this about their wives. And yet… After an energetic and satisfying round of sex, they turned on their respective sides and went to sleep. Charlie had always thought it was great that Lorena didn't need to talk to death, like women do after sex. Now, he was not sure this was beneficial to their marriage. Perhaps a little cuddling and talking about their day would have been better.

Lorena turned. "Hey Charlie! Billy Bob told me everything went great today. I'm so glad it's over…" She came to hug him.

"Billy Bob shouldn't have had to tell you this…" He stopped her.

"Now, don't be ridiculous! You're not mad because I didn't come, are you? I understand there were a lot of people there."

"That's right. A lot of people, but not you."

"Charlie! I hope you're not going to bear a grudge for this. I couldn't come and face Wilma and all those accusing people."

"You're not even going to pretend you were busy with your catering business, are you?"

"Well sure. That too."

Charlie shook his head in wonder. When Lorena thought she was right, no matter how obvious the reality was, she was strong in her beliefs.

"I'm disappointed," he added and left the kitchen.

The next day found Charlie on Main Street, near Starbucks, where he had dropped off some papers for Michael. The Country Club had left the place in a hurry, perhaps caused by Michael's promise that otherwise they'll ask for an investigation into their finances. The members paid a hefty annual fee and the rent had not been paid for three years. The money simply had vanished. Also, Mahoney, the president disappeared together with all his papers overnight.

Michael suggested that Charlie keep Kevin, owner of the Bright Blooms nursery to take care of the grounds and Kevin offered his cousin, who was an accountant, to temporaryly manage the newly independent Golf Club.

"Charlie!" a cheerful voice called out from behind him.

Oh joy! The high school principal. "Murphy!" Charlie said curtly, trying to pass by.

"Call me Don, please. We're all friends here in Hunters Crossing."

"Are we? I wonder!"

"Of course, of course. Everyone is asking when you could resume coaching the football team. They all miss you."

"Well, I don't want to be a…'nefarious influence' – as you said."

"Ah man, that is water under the bridge. All was clarified. The judge himself said so. We'll see you at the stadium." Principal Murphy grabbed and shook Charlie's hand vigorously and left.

Charlie looked after him in wonder. This guy should be a politician to be able to flip his position with so much ease and grace, as if there was no harm done, no vicious words said.

He opened his truck's door and was trying to avoid Scruffy's overly enthusiastic welcome kisses when his phone rang. He missed Floria like crazy, and his heart was boken. Thinking it was her calling, he answered immediately.

"Hello Charlie. This is Tony Darnell from New York. I haven't heard from you in a while and our baseball show project is on track, financing and all. We tried other narrators and we all agreed your voice is the best. Not only the tone, but you talk in a sincere, convincing way and it's clear you know what you're talking about, not only reading what's in front of you. So, I thought to ask you again, are you on or not. I'm afraid I need the answer now."

Charlie thought how empty he felt after Floria had left, how everybody went on with their every day life, how Drew would leave soon for college and Amanda would leave to her life in Washington DC, how Lorena and his father were involved with the catering business. He felt so alone and without motivation. "I'm on," he heard himself saying.

"Great, I'm glad to hear. When can you come?"

Charlie met Scruffy's questioning eyes. "I'm flexible in terms of time, accommodation and all. But I have a dog, and he comes where I go. I don't know if…"

Tony laughed. "It so happens that I too have a mutt that I adore. We were prepared to offer hotel, but if you don't mind bunking with me in my loft, we could walk the dogs together to the nearby small park."

"Great, see you soon, Tony."

Back at home, Charlie went straight to the kitchen where Lorena and Billy Bob, surrounded by a lot of platters with all sorts of tiny foods, were taking a break with a tea pot between them.

"Hello the kitchen!" Charlie said, taking a seat at the table.

"Charlie, do you want a sandwich?" his father asked, always so helpful nowadays.

"No, thank you. I need to talk to you both. I don't know if you are aware that the Country Club doesn't exist any longer."

"Oh yes. That crooked Mahoney ran away with the money," Lorena said. "Violet called and told me. I was stunned. Mahoney was such a nice, distinguished man…Who would have thought?"

"You talked friendly with Violet as if nothing had happened?" Charlie interrupted.

"Well, of course. She'd been upset over the incident like everybody else, but now…"

Charlie was more and more amazed by how easily people could pretend that no harm was done by snubbing, patronizing, and even insulting the other person. Was he the only crazy one who could not get over this? "What you choose to do Lorena is your business, but I will tell you that Victor is not welcome in my house any longer. This is not a passing whim. In my mind, he betrayed our friendship and I can't trust him anymore. Not negotiable."

Lorena wanted to argue, but there was a more pressing matter on her mind. "Charlie, she said that you own the Country Club. How is it possible?"

"I don't own the Country Club. I own a company CC Development that buys and develops or rents buildings, land, and so on. So yes, I own the land and the buildings, together with other buildings in town, and several pieces of land. Just because I don't advertise this, doesn't mean it's a secret. I told you several times that we are financially secure. I'm by no means one of the wealthiest in the country, but I suppose I am the richest man in town. The funny thing is Lyle Mendoza is the only one that might come close in fortune."

"Wow, and you never told me?"

"I did, but you chose not to believe me."

"I thought that we had some of your retirement money. I feared that with any downturn in the economy, we could be penniless."

"You chose to let your childhood fears of poverty overcome my assurances. My fortune is spread in a variety of investments that can not all fail."

Lorena considered this in silence, while Billy Bob was smiling. Charlie knew that Billy Bob was astute enough to have known all along.

"Anyhow, I have something I want to discuss with both of you. I have a manager for the Golf Club. The old Country Club, renamed for the moment the Hunters Crossing Community Club, will be accessible to anyone who wants to cater a party, wedding, and other activities like conferences, not to mention to use the tennis court or even a small library. There will need to be a fee for all this, to assure the maintenance of the grounds and building. I need a good, trustworthy manager, and also creative with the Club activities and possibilities. I thought of the two of you. I never thought in a million years of a more strange partnership, but it seems to work for the two of you, so who am I to argue."

Billy Bob gripped his tea mug. "Well, I was thinking that my visit had been long enough and I should go back to Florida to visit my widow. Maybe time made her miss me."

Lorena looked at him horrified. "Billy Bob, how do you think I could manage the catering business without you, not to mention the new Club. I can't compete with Florida, but I need you. How about you stay another 'indefinite' period until we make all these businesses work?"

"It's a balm to be needed at my age, so if you want me to, I'll stay a little longer."

Lorena rose and brought to the table some papers. "I registered the catering business officially at the Chamber of Commerce and I named both of us as partners. Now you have a vested interest to stay. "

They shook hands and Billy Bob had tears in his eyes. "And you Charlie, what will you do? Go back to coaching the high school football team?" his father asked.

"Maybe, but not this season. I am going to New York to host a TV show about baseball. A guy I knew in my playing days is producing it and asked me to narrate it."

"New York City? That's splendid!" Lorena

exclaimed.

"Would you like to come too?" Charlie asked with curiosity.

Lorena had a wistful look in her eyes, masked quickly by determination. "No, I couldn't. The many businesses need me here."

Charlie didn't bother to say that if she wanted to be with him, they could hire managers for both businesses or take a break from the catering. He knew her wistful look was for visiting New York City, not for being with him. "So be it. We're all set." There was nothing more to say.

CHAPTER 24

After trying on several outfits, under Lorena's critical eyes, Amanda settled on the first one, a simple, black cashmere dress with long sleeves. The dress followed the neckline, but the soft fabric molded to her generous breasts and tiny waist and was sexier than any others with more revealing décolletage. Lorena added a red belt and a long row of small iridescent pearls.

Amanda looked critically in the mirror. "I don't know about the pearls. In the DC circles they are considered 'passé', old fashion Nancy Reagan sort of thing."

"Possible. But my mama always told me 'you place pearls on an old tired dress and it will be elegant' and my mama knew what she was saying. Besides, this is not DC, this is Hunters Crossing and I bet Lyle Mendoza won't know or care pearls are out of fashion this year," Lorena argued.

It was true. The pearls added an understated sort of elegance to the plain black dress.

179

"Don't you think they swing too much on my chest?" Amanda asked.

"Oh honey, they sure do swing. That's the idea."

Not convinced she had the best outfit, Amanda had some anxiety while waiting for Lyle to come pick her up. Unlike Lorena, she knew Lyle was not a country bumpkin, unable to appreciate true elegance. Lorena herself had been a bit mollified in her opinions about Lyle, after finding out that he was rich. Amanda eyed her expensive Jimmy Choos and hoped Lyle will not come in a small low sports car, like so many men in DC, who wanted to impress their dates. If only they knew how uncomfortable was for a woman to squeeze herself in, trying to keep her skirts decent and her stockings intact, without a run.

Lyle came in a nice, comfortable SUV, which was new judging by the smell of the leather seats inside. Sighing happily, Amanda climbed in. Lyle himself was dressed in black slacks and a cashmere dark blue pullover with an immaculate white shirt underneath. She was glad she chose the pearls. He looked very elegant with his long black trench coat.

"We have to drive a way. The restaurant is in the outskirts of Cincinnati. But it will be worth the drive, you'll see. The food is pretty good," Lyle said.

"We don't have to go that far…"

"Don't worry, I talked to Charlie and he knows where we are."

After driving for half an hour or so, they left the main road and followed a narrowed road through the woods. Right when Amanda thought they were lost, a lighted sign announced The English Manor. A large Edwardian building was bordered on both sides by parking lots. Lyle drove first at the very edge of the right lot, showing her the view from there. There was a panoramic view of the valley, with thousands of lights of the city bellow.

"Oh my God, it's so beautiful. During the day, it must be truly spectacular."

Lyle laughed. "I'll bring you here during the day too," he promised.

The interior was very luxurious, with huge crystal

chandeliers, old carved wood, and alcoves with tables covered in white tablecloths. The Maitre d' led them to one such alcove near the window. "Mr. Mendoza, your table, sir."

"Lyle," Amanda whispered. "I am impressed, but for a first date, we could have gone to Mama Sophia, the premier Italian restaurant in Hunters Crossing. I didn't expect all this."

"I'll take you to Mama Sophia next time if that is what your heart desires." Lyle smiled showing his dimples.

The food was divine and they talked about everything from childhood stories to movies, books, music, and hobbies. When the scrumptious desert came, Amanda was mellowed by the good food and the three glasses of various wines she'd tasted.

"I still don't understand why you picked me?" she asked curious.

"Why not you?" Lyle set his glass on the table.

"Oh, I don't know. I'm average, with brown hair, brown eyes, and average height. Not ugly, but definitely not beautiful enough to turn heads."

He considered his words. "Amanda, I'm thirty-eight years old. I achieved my professional goals, which consumed me to obsession all my youth. I was driven. Now, I still work hard, but I slowed down a little my driving ambition. I discovered that I don't like being alone. No matter what Charlie thinks about me, and he threatened to cut my…throat if I hurt you, I don't like playing the field. I'm ready to settle down. I know all the women available in Hunters Crossing and the nearby vicinity. While some are remarkable and beautiful, they don't fit me."

"Ah, the quest for the perfect wife," Amanda said, a little tipsy. That would not be her. At twenty-seven, she was nowhere near ready to settle down in the matrimonial bliss. She still had professional success to achieve. Too bad. Lyle seemed to be an interesting guy, not to say splendid looking. But no marriage for her, thank you. Unless…

"Not the perfect wife, Amanda," he corrected her, smiling. "Not the trophy wife, but the right one for me, with physical chemistry…" He caressed her hand, sending shivers of excitement down her spine and muddling her thoughts. "…sex is important. The right woman for me needs to be intelligent so I can enjoy talking to her, but not a genius for an average Joe like me. And to be loyal and faithful and supportive, as I intend to be in return."

Amanda tried to clear her mind. She had this idea that might, just might work. "Listen Lyle, I have an idea. I knew from the moment I saw you that you were perfect. Listen! I worked as political advisor to Senator Smith…"

"Who resigned…"

"Yes well, that was unfortunate, but I am good at what I do…"

"If you are worried I'm going to try to stop you from working…."

"No, no. That's not it. I have this brilliant idea. I could help you win a Senate seat. You are perfect. Self-made, working hard to succeed, honest, not a Washington insider. We could do it." Her eyes sparkled with excitement. She grabbed his hand, more and more taken with this image.

His face showed first amazement and then disbelief. "You want me to run for a Senate seat?"

"Why, yes. With the right campaign, I'm pretty sure you will succeed to get elected. Right age and profile, right platform…."

His eyes narrowed and he pulled his hand from hers. "Amanda, stop right there. You thought of this the minute you saw me?"

"Yes, it crossed my mind that you would be perfect," she answered hesitating and aware that he was not as enthusiastic as she presumed he would be.

He shook his head. "Wow, talk about mistaking the signals. I don't want to be liked for my looks only, but I guess I was vain and thought you liked me as I liked you and wanted to get to know me better."

"But I do, I like you very much and….,"she protested.

"Amanda, I don't have any interest to be a politician. I like my life the way it is now. I am known as the Trashman, did you know that?"

"I do and this is not an impediment…."

"I want to be accepted the way I am."

"I do, I accept you as you are. I admire you."

Lyle shook his head again. "No you don't. You want to play Pygmalion and transform me into what I'm not, a political figure, with a permanent fake smile on my face, with an agenda very different from what he promised. The funny thing is, I thought you were so genuine, fresh, and different from most other people." He placed the desert fork on his plate and signaled the waiter for the bill. "We all live and learn, I guess."

Amanda had a hard time understanding what went wrong. "But Lyle, I wanted what's best for you…"

"And you think you know what's best for me?" He was not angry now, only sad. Amanda wanted to make it better. To kiss him and take away the sadness, but he was building a wall between them, a wall of formal politeness. "Do you want coffee?" he asked.

"No, thank you," she answered, although she would have loved a strong coffee to clear her brain.

And that was that. He walked her to the car, with

the same unfailing politeness and opened the door and helped her get into the SUV. On the rather long drive back, to chase away the oppressive silence, Amanda tried to make conversation.

"This was an amazing place. How did you discover it?"

"I was driving to Cincinnati and I always like to drive the back roads, to explore the country, when I came upon this place with its amazing views. The house was dilapidated and the 'For Sale" sign was buried in the weeds. I bought it for a fraction of the value, and restored it when I could and when I had extra money. Then I met a very good chef. His culinary creations were famous. He was slavering in a second hand restaurant, waiting to have enough money to start his own business. We are partners. He is master in the kitchen and I supervise the rest, the building, the gardens, finances, prices and so on. We also have a large outdoor space we use in the summer."

"Oh my God, you own that beautiful place!" Amanda said. He didn't answer.

After a while she tried again, "Lyle, my brain is scrambled after three glasses of wine. I'm sorry if my idea was not good for you, but I like you very much and I would like to know you better. Could we please meet again?"

"I don't mean to be inflexible. I just don't think we are right for each other," he said after a brief hesitation.

When the car stopped in front of Charlie's house, he accompanied her politely to the door. "Good bye, Amanda."

She looked at him through tears and daring him said, "What, no Good bye kiss?"

He laughed at that. "Let it not be said I disappointed a lady."

He took her in his arms and Amanda clung to him and the kiss was devastating, sweet and passionate and powerful.

But it ended and he left her there without another word.

CHAPTER 25

Charlie was caught in a whirlwind of preparations for his upcoming travel to New York. Not his preparations. He would take only a small carry on bag, determined to buy all he needed in New York. For Scruffy however, he needed a lot; papers, proof of vaccinations, special carrier and a lot of other things and arrangements with the airline.

He was surprised to find Amanda in the family room in an armchair, looking out the window and lost in thought. "Amanda!" he called. Her face was wet with tears.

"I'll kill him. I told him not to hurt you. I'll cut his…well, throat." Charlie ranted enraged.

"No Charlie. You see, it was my fault."

"How can it be your fault? Even if it were, as a gentleman he should apologize to make it all right."

"No, it was my fault. I had this crazy idea that he is perfect to run for a seat."

"A seat where?"

"A seat in the Senate. The old Senator is retiring."

Charlie scratched his head. "You thought Lyle should be a Senator? You see honey, Lyle is a small town boy at heart. As successful as he is and wealthy, he likes it here, playing pool with the boys at Lou's Tavern, and picking up trash when his company needs him."

"Yes, I know that, but he'd have been elected if he chose to run for office."

"He'd be utterly miserable in the distinguished company of senators and the like."

Amanda nodded. "I understand that now, but it's too late."

"Why? What's the problem? He said 'No, thanks' and …"

"He decided we don't suit each other. Oh Charlie! What am I going to do?" Amanda wailed. "After we parted I thought of all this and I realized that perhaps I was upset to be jobless. I wanted to prove I am good at what I do and can 'make' a political career. It's all true, but I think I want Lyle more."

"That settles it," Charlie said, standing up from

the nearby chair. "If it's Lyle you want, then I'll get him for you. Although, I admit he has a pretty face, I don't see why women are making all the fuss around him. 'Pretty is as pretty does' – they say."

"He is so much more than a pretty face. He is caring and gentle, hard-working and ambitious, loyal and nice."

"I'm sure he's a bundle of virtues," Charlie puffed.

"…and he makes me tingle all over…."

"He dared to touch you?"

"On my hand."

"Oh, okay then."

"And when he kissed me…," Amanda continued dreamily.

"That's it. I'll kill him."

"…it was earth-shattering."

Charlie sat back in the chair. "All right, I'll get him for you."

"You can't do that, Charlie. He decided he doesn't want me."

"And then he kissed you. I'm sorry but in my book it says he wants you."

Amanda looked at him with a little hope in her eyes. "Do you think so? You know I dared him to kiss me."

"A man who doesn't want a woman will say 'No. thank you'. Especially if he doesn't want complications....You know, Amanda, once a very smart person told me that Romeo and Juliet were stupid people for failing to communicate. I think you should go out there and tell him that you care and want him and force him to acknowledge that he cares too."

Amanda sniffed and bent to pet Scruffy who came to see what all the ruckus was about. "You know, I think I will."

"But be very sure that you want him. Don't play games."

She nodded. "I am sure. I know that now."

It was a Saturday night at Lou's Tavern and the regulars were all there, except Charlie, who was busy making last minute arrangements for his absence.

This time, a band was singing in a corner and the customers were clapping in rhythm. In the back room, Oscar Tramontana was trying his luck positioning the cue, but could not hit the ball successfully. Tony Mendoza was cheering him on and Ken and Lyle were throwing darts. A whole bunch of females were gathered around, all sighing and glancing at Lyle. Doris, the singer was plastered all over him. It was a wonder he succeeded to throw the darts with such precision.

Then the cheers stopped. Tramontana pushed his cue through the felt of the billiard table. Tony Mendoza, his eyes glued on the entrance said: "Oh Lord, she's gorgeous!" Ken gave up trying to impress Doris, who was not interested in him anyway, and took a big gulp of his beer while looking at the newcomer.

The woman slowly took off her coat, revealing a short red dress very tight on her curves. Her hair was brown and curly, reaching the middle of her back. She had a lot of make-up on. Were those fake eyelashes, she was fluttering at Tony when he tried to help with her trench coat? She smiled with her very red lips at him and Tony stumbled over his own feet.

She advanced moving her hips and taking the cue from Tramontana, she bent and all men sighed watching mesmerized the long legs encased in black stockings, not to mention the round bottom barely covered in that red flimsy fabric. Lyle realized he'd broken the tail of his dart. Disgusted, he threw it on the floor.

Meanwhile, the woman, with an experienced move of the cue sent the right ball in the corner net. Not that anybody was paying attention to that. They were all entranced by the red covered curves.

Then, she turned and slowly approached Lyle. "Hello Lyle!" she said in a throaty voice.

Doris, the singer, was the first to recover her poise. Clutching his arm she asked, "Who do you think you are?"

The woman, dislodging Doris' fingers from Lyle's arm, said, "I'm Amanda and he's mine. All mine."

"So you say," Doris protested. "But he's not interested."

"If he's not, then I am," Ken said, raising his hand to touch the backside curve, clad in red.

"Don't you dare touch her or I'll break your fingers," Lyle growled in a menacing voice.

And just like that, Amanda threw her head backwards and laughed. A joyous, happy laugh.

"Let's get out of here," Lyle pronounced and grabbing her hand pulled her to the exit.

CHAPTER 26

Everything was set. Charlie was traveling the next day to New York. Upstairs, in the bedroom, he was inspecting for the last time his carry on luggage and checked his list of issues to address before leaving. Scruffy, lying on the small rug near the bed was resting after a big meal of his favorite Kibbles'n Bits, not knowing that he would have to experience several hours in a carrier in the luggage compartment. For the moment he was content to be here in the bedroom with Charlie.

It had been a long fight for Scruffy. First, he had been banished to the laundry/mud room. His howling protests all night long convinced Lorena to allow him in Charlie's office. This worked during the day, but at night, he emitted such lugubrious whining that in the end Lorena accepted it would be easier to let him sleep near Charlie's bed. And it was easier. Scruffy made no noise all night long and they all had uninterrupted sleep. That was, except when Charlie needed to go to the bathroom and quite sleepy, forgot the dog was there and

196

accidentally stumbled over him.

Ding, dong!

Charlie wanted to ignore the bell ringing, but Lorena was at the Club and the person at the door was persistent.

Ding, dong!

"You stay here, Scruffy! I'll send the person on his way and be right back."

Ding, dong!

"I'm coming, I'm coming." These days, his house was like Central Station busy with all the people coming and going, people with business for Lorena, classmates for Drew, lovesick Lyle for Amanda, and friends for all of them, who seemed to have multiplied lately. Charlie was glad he was leaving. Lorena embraced them open-hearted, but he was ambiguous about their presence in his house.

He opened the door. Waiting there was a girl, who looked to be about sixteen years old, maybe a little older, but not by much. She had short spiked black hair, the tips colored purple, and big, blue innocent eyes in total contrast with the Halloweenish hair. She clutched the hand of a small boy, maybe four years old, with the same big blue eyes and blond curly hair. The adorable cherub held in his other hand a tattered stuffed giraffe.

"Mr. Callahan? I'm Madeline Jones and this is Max. I would like fifteen minutes of your time to talk to you about an important issue. Please!"

Charlie inclined his head and motioned for them to enter. Once news of his wealth status spread in town, quite a few people had approached him asking for help, monetary or influential. This girl seemed familiar. Her jeans were torn at the knee, but nowadays one didn't know if it was poverty or a fashionable designer style. Same thing for the too long shirt, hanging from under the shorter pullover. If she wanted his help, he'd do it for the charming little boy.

He guided them to the living-room, a place totally useless in Charlie's opinion. The all-white look, - the designer had insisted was all the rage and very classy, - looked like a hospital and the leather furniture, sofa and chairs were equally uninviting and cold.

STORM IN A GLASS OF WATER

The girl sat gingerly on the edge of the sofa. The little boy climbed up near her and placed his giraffe nearby. He looked at Charlie with big, round eyes, unblinking and serious like a little owl. Charlie wondered if he needed glasses. He took a seat in a chair, facing them across the glass coffee table. "What can I do for you?"

The girl's voice trembled a little when she spoke. Charlie wondered if she'd rehearsed her story. "When I was young…," she started. How young was young for her, in kindergarten? "…at my prom graduation…," she continued.

"Pardon me! How old are you?" Charlie interrupted.

"I am twenty-four. I was in June…. So, at my prom party I was invited by one of the popular boys in school. Very happy, my grandmother and I worked all night long to finish sewing the dress. I lived with my grandmother, you see, she raised me after my mother left me. I never knew my father. We lived in the poor neighborhood in the east, but I was happy with her. I knew I was loved, you see. Not many kids abandoned or not, are lucky to feel they are loved." She wiped a tear from her eyes, smudging a little her mascara. "Anyhow, the prom was not my dream come true. My girlfriends made fun of my beautiful dress. They knew it was home-made, you see, and my date... It turned out he invited me to make jealous some other girl and he abandoned me. I decided to leave early. There was no reason to stay. I started to walk slowly home. At some point, a car stopped near me. I recognized the driver as one of the most popular guys in school, Rob Callahan."

"My Rob? You mean my son?" Charlie asked.

"Yes. I don't know why he left early. I suppose he had a fight with his girlfriend. He offered me a ride and I gladly climbed into his car. We talked about all sorts of things, plans for the future, him going to college. He knew right then he wanted to go to medical school. I had no plans and no money for college, but I told him my secret desire was to sing. After talking in front of my house, he asked me if I wanted to see the moon from the lake side. There was a full moon that night. I agreed and we drove into the wooded area east of town, near the lake. We were very comfortable talking and sharing silly personal thoughts. That night Max was conceived."

Charlie thought his hearing was defective all of a sudden. "Say that again?"

She swallowed and enunciated clearly, "Max is Rob's son."

"But... but how is this possible? Are you telling me Rob ... forced..."

The girl shook her head. "No, no. It was something we both wanted. To chase away the memory of a failed prom and unworthy dates. The joy of having someone to share the personal dreams. It was a beautiful night. But only one night. We both knew he had to go to college and next day I would be the same girl from the poor side of town."

Charlie looked at the quiet kid. It was such an incredible story he felt poleaxed. The kid had his mother's eyes. Still looking back at him, the kid scrunched his nose in a familiar way that reminded him of both his boys when they were little. But, a scrunched nose did not make a blood relation. "How come we, his family, didn't know?"

"It was Rob's decision not to tell anybody. He asked me to keep secret his paternity and I did what he asked." She looked at him with understanding and for the first time smiled. She searched through her purse and produced a thin manila envelope. "Here, take it. Rob didn't deny Max was his, but as soon as Max was one year old, I insisted on DNA testing. This is it. Without doubt." She pushed the envelope towards Charlie.

"Young lady you know how to deliver punches, what can I say?"

"I didn't mean to, sir. I never asked Rob for anything. I knew he was busy with his college. Another world, and a new girlfriend. He came when he could, not very often. He helped with some money now and again…. My grandmother took care of Max, when I went to work. He is a very good boy."

The very good boy opened his mouth and pronounced in a very firm voice for one so small, "Fannie is thirsty."

The girl shushed him embarrassed, "Sh..sh..Max. Fannie is the giraffe," she explained.

"Oh, excuse me." Charlie said and went to the kitchen. He came back with a plate with cookies and a carafe with orange juice. The little boy shook his head at the cookies, drank half a glass of juice, wiped his mouth with his sleeve before his mother reached for a napkin and smiled a nice, mischievous smile at Charlie. "Tank yo." And just like that Charlie lost his heart to this little human being, DNA or no DNA.

The girl sipped a little from her own glass, daintily wiped her mouth and continued, "Three months ago, my grandmother died. She was only sixty nine, but I guess a lifetime of hard work took its toll. She had a heart attack and just like that she was gone," she started sobbing softly. "I tried to make it work. In addition to my cashier's job at the grocery store I started singing in bars, at Lou's Tavern."

"Lou's Tavern?" That's why she looked familiar to Charlie.

She nodded. "I tried everything. I took Max with

me at work. He is really a good boy, never complains, always quiet, with his books and toys. I leave him with my neighbor when she's free, but I don't have money for a babysitter and it is unfair to Max. I am a good mother and I love him very much, but things can't go on like this." She sniffed. "A month ago a country music band stopped at Lou's Tavern. They needed a lead singer and we clicked. We blended very well our singing styles. They went on to Nashville. They emailed me asking me to join them there. I'm not naïve to believe I'll become a celebrity overnight. There is plenty of unnoticed talent in Nashville, but I think I have a chance to earn money doing what I like. Singing is all I know."

"You want to take Max to Nashville?" Charlie asked horrified by this perspective.

The girl, Madeline laughed. "Nashville is not a den of vice. But no, I don't intend to take him with me. He deserves a normal little boy childhood, with his family who loves him. I have no doubt they'll love him."

"What family?" Charlie asked.

Madeline looked down in her lap, picking at a

loose thread. "Well, I'm sorry to spring this on you, but I know you are a good man Charlie Callahan, loyal, honest….I can't think of a better guardian for Max."

"Wait a minute young woman, these things are not so simple."

"Sure they are." She took out another envelope from her purse. "I visited that nice attorney, Michael Fraser, and here are papers giving you full, sole custody of Max. He is yours. I raised him for four years. He knows he has a mama who loves him. Now it's your turn. I trust you. I wouldn't trust Rob to take care of him and frankly I'm not sure about your wife either. But I trust you. You understand what a treasure Max is. I only ask to be allowed to see him once in a while when I come back." She pushed the second envelope to Charlie. "You have here everything. Birth certificate, medical records, and the custody papers."

Charlie looked at the little boy. "Maxwell?"

The girl corrected him. "It's Maximilian Charles Jones. Named after his two grandfathers. If you want to adopt him and change his last name to Callahan I have no objection."

"Max? It suits him. Max, do you want to stay here with us?" he asked the little boy. If he expected a shy, 'eyes downcast, hiding behind mama's skirts', response he was wrong. The boy looked straight at him, pondering his answer, then said in the same firm voice as before: "Max wants doggy."

Charlie looked at the girl for clarification. She shushed the boy again. "It's nothing. You see, he always wanted to have a dog. He ran after all the strays. It doesn't matter."

"He wants a dog, hmm?" Charlie looked at the boy, who was prepared to negotiate some more, by the look of stubbornness on his face. Same as Rob, when he wanted something. No temper tantrum, no hysterical cries, only a stubborn persistence.

The boy nodded and repeated, "Max wants doggy." Then he gave the strongest argument he could think of, "And Fannie wants doggy." He waved the giraffe with vigor. Charlie was afraid the stuffing will spread all over Lorena's elegant white décor. And who knew when the Merry Maids were supposed to come. Although now, with a child in the house, they'll be needed more frequently.

Charlie turned to Madeline. "I suppose it's pointless to say 'be careful, a young girl alone in a big city can't be too cautious'. And of course I want to help you start with some money until you…"

"No, no please," Madeline interrupted. "I can't deny I don't have any money and I desperately need some, and thank you for offering, but I can't accept. It will be like selling Max and it's not true. I love him and I want the best for him. Somehow I'll manage, singing here and there. Don't worry. The band will take care of me. They are good guys." She embraced Max holding him tightly, then kissed Charlie on the cheek, whispering, "Take good care of him." And then she was gone.

Charlie looked at Max for any signs of panic, but there were none. He clutched the giraffe to him and said, "Mama had to go, Fannie. She'd have stayed if she could, but she had to go." Then he raised his eyes to Charlie.

Charlie put out his hand and said: "Now, it's you and me, partner. And I promised you a doggy." Max considered this and slowly placed his small hand in Charlie's.

They went in the entryway and Charlie whistled, "Scruffy, come here boy."

Scruffy came galloping downstairs, skidding all over the marble floor, and halting in front of the little boy. Max laughed and embraced the crazy mutt, trying to avoid having his face licked.

They would be fine. Charlie thought. It had been an agitated year, but they'd be fine.

CHAPTER 27

Email from Charles Callahan to Floria Hunter-Clark

Dear Flori,

I just came from Michael's office. I convinced him to move into a better building I own on Main Street. You remember the old man Stavros' New and Used Bookstore. It is right across the street from Weinstein & Krantz Attorneys. By the way, Krantz left for parts unknown, some say Florida Keys. Weinstein is alone and with not too much business. Anyhow, I moved Michael in place of the old bookstore that closed. (I'm so sorry about that. Stavros couldn't stop the e-readers from taking away his business.) Now Michael is the acclaimed attorney to go to in Hunters Crossing.

My life, as I wrote to you before, changed completely. Max is a delight. He and Scruffy make my life worth living. I'm upset that Rob is not more interested in Max. The years are flying by and then it will be too late. But what can I do?

Lorena is very busy. She hired more personnel for her catering business and seems
more involved in managing the Club.

Amanda left for Washington DC, but returned soon after to spend the Christmas and New Year with us. She and Drew adore little Max and like to play with him. I don't dare to ask her how her relationship with Lyle is going. I think all's well as they are together all the time.

I miss you Flori, more than I can say. I hope I'll see you soon. If you're not too busy with your friends and various clubs, please come to visit me.

Yours always, Charlie

Email from Floria Hunter-Clark to Charlie Callahan,

Darling Charlie,

I adore these new ways of communicating. Your phone call yesterday made me so happy. I was at the Bridge Club and went outside to hear you better. My cell is an old flip phone. Maybe I should change it with a new one.

Look dearest, another year went by in a blink and we are getting older. Ha-ha, just joking. I plan to come this summer to Hunters Crossing, perhaps for the 4th of July celebration. I would like to meet Max while he is still little and before he becomes a teenager.

Listen, I want to tell you something amusing. Yesterday morning, I was at the grocery store and when I finished, I realized that my car, four years old with only 2500 miles on it, won't start. I turned the key on and off and on again. Nothing. The darned car didn't want to start. I checked not to have left it in Drive instead of the Park position. (It happened to me some other time.) All good. I got out of the car, turned around it, not knowing what to do. Then I got in trying again to start it. Nothing. I was looking in the glove box for an Emergency number, when I saw that the owner of the motorcycle parked nearby had returned. He was one of those bikers, dressed all in leather, tattooed, with long black hair tied with a bandanna. Who do they think they are? Geronimo?

Now I was desperate to leave, turning the key, and willing the stupid car to start. No such luck. Then he knocked on my window. I thought I'd faint for sure. I pretended not to hear, but he persisted. So, I opened the window only a tiny bit. 'Ma'am, could you please open the hood, so I could see what's wrong with your car?' he said. I thought – what harm could he do – the engine was dead anyhow. I fumbled a bit. I had no idea which button to press to open the hood. He laughed and pointed to the right button. When the hood opened, he went to the front of the car, did something there, and then motioned to me to start the engine again. I did and miracle! It started immediately. I was so grateful. I forgot my fear and got out of the car to thank him and to offer him some money for his effort.

And Charlie dearest, you will not believe what happened. He rejected my money offer, seemed even offended by it, and then smiled and said that as payment we could have lunch at a Thai bistro in the neighborhood. I was so shocked. I didn't know what to say. He saw I hesitated and said he'll wait for me there tomorrow at noon. And then he rode his bike away.

Now Charlie, why do you think a biker, probably ten years younger than me, wants to have lunch with me?

I wanted to email you this to have a good laugh at my adventures.

All my love, Floria

Email from Charlie Callahan to Floria Hunter-Clark

Dear Floria,

I read your email with some anxiety. The world is full of nutcases and crooks. Please be very careful. You are a special person, lovely, adorable and any man would enjoy your company. I would be the first to advise you to have a little fun. However a biker, ten years younger, really! I mean even if he's not a danger to you, I don't see how you could connect with him or even enjoy a simple lunch. What could you two possibly talk about?

Be careful dear, I worry for you, Charlie

Email from Floria Hunter-Clark to Charlie

Callahan,

Dearest Charlie,

You'll be happy to know your fears were for nothing. After agonizing all night long, I decided to go to the Thai Bistro if for nothing else, but to thank him for his help. It turns out he is a mechanic with his own garage business. He gave me his card in case I might need him in the future. He was very polite and I think he saw me only in terms of a prospective customer, although he said I had pretty eyes.

So you see, no danger, no flirt, nothing. Story of my life.

Darling, I will come this summer for sure to see you. My life is very satisfying, but quite predictable, and I feel a strange restlessness growing. Oh well, traveling to Hunters Crossing will be great.

Love, Floria

EPILOGUE

That 4th of July celebration was an event to remember a long time after by the citizens of Hunters Crossing. The newly elected Mayor Charlie Callahan had supervised all the preparations. He organized the parade with marching bands, floats and all; this was scheduled in the morning on Main Street. Also, after months of hard, volunteer work, the park at Silver Lake looked great, with picnic tables, lawn for kids to play and run and a softball space. For the Independence Day, there was an improvised stage for a band to play and plenty of space all-around for people to watch the fireworks later that night.

People were determined to have an unforgettable, splendid celebration and to enjoy themselves. They also had a lot to talk about. Like when the First Lady of Hunters Crossing, Mrs. Lorena Callahan, beautiful and graceful as always, who was preparing to announce the start of the parade, turned to her husband, with worry in her eyes.

"Charlie! Stop feeding the dog, Max is doing enough of that already. Look at those people, those scary bikers! Do you think someone hired them to spoil our festivities?"

Charlie looked across the street in the parking lot, where the bikers had stopped. Sure enough there was this big guy, with long dark hair, a bandanna tied on top of his head, a black leather vest, showing a multitude of colorful tattoos on his arms. The other one, short and round, pulled the helmet off and a crown of short golden hair shined in the sun. Oh, the good Lord, what was she doing on the bike? She placed her small hand on the guy's muscled tattooed arm, listening to what he said and laughed; a spontaneous, joyful burst of laughter.

All around the Mayor and his wife, people had quieted down, looking from them to the fierce looking biker and his companion. The Mayor patted his wife's hand in assurance. "These, my dear, are my special guests, Mr. Wayne Prescott from Rancho Bernardo, California and his fiancée, Floria Hunter-Clark."

And people, reassured too, started cheering as the

high school marching band opened the parade and the celebration continued.

The day had a lot of other memorable moments. Like later in the afternoon, in the park, people were sitting on blankets, lawn chairs or the picnic benches, enjoying the country music band and the newly launched, talented singer Madeline Jones.

Right then, little Max climbed in the Mayor's lap and shouted for all to hear, "That is my Mama!" pointing clearly at the singer, whose voice trembled and stopped. The moment was saved by the band that played their drums louder to cover the incident.

If people hoped for a good gossipy subject, they were disappointed. The Mayor's wife took the child in her arms and laughing, kissed him and bumped noses with him. It was clear she loved the child adopted by the Mayor when he was four years old. Besides the child was adorable, and everybody loved him. Oh well, no source of scandal here, it seemed.

The evening went on with the splendid fireworks show exploding over the lake in a myriad of colorful tiny stars.

And in the noise surrounding them all, nobody heard the Mayor asking in a whispering tone, "Are you happy, Flori?"

The answer came in an equally hushed tone, but without hesitation, "Oh yes! Yes, I am."

* * *

STORM IN A GLASS OF WATER

For news about recently published books by Vivian Sinclair and upcoming new ones visit Vivian's website at viviansinclairbooks.com

A Walk In The Rain, a contemporary women's fiction novel

The Virginia Lovers Trilogy:

Book 1 – Alexandra's Garden

Book 2 – Ariel's Summer Vacation

Book 3 – Lulu's Christmas Wish

Western contemporary romance books:

A Guest At The Ranch

The Maitland Legacy, A Family Saga series:

Book 1 – Lost in Wyoming (Lance's story)

Book 2 – Moon Over Laramie (Tristan's story)

Book 3 – Christmas In Cheyenne (Raul's story)

Turn the page and keep reading for and excerpt from A Walk In The Rain, a contemporary women's fiction novel.

A Walk In The Rain

Rain

VIVIAN SINCLAIR

CHAPTER 1

It was a cold rainy day in October, similar to many other days in the long wet season in the Pacific Northwest.

It was also the day when Miranda Henderson discovered that two of her most valuable possessions were missing.

The first one, a Chihuli glass bowl had been an anniversary present from her late husband Bob, who had bought it from the Museum of Glass in Tacoma for $15,000. He had done this grudgingly, arguing that to invest money in glass and live in an earthquake prone area was a bad idea. He was right, but Miranda had been fascinated with the bowl, which reflected the light in a rainbow of colors and iridescent swirls. She kept it on the small table near the sofa where she rested every afternoon and felt the bowl was magical. Every time she was anxious, upset or a little depressed, touching the bowl and looking at it never failed to bring her calm and peace of mind.

The second object missing was an abstract painting that Bob had acquired from an art dealer in Kirkland few years ago, paying only $2,000. Two thousand too many, as far as Miranda was concerned. It was an 'angry' painting, she thought. Deep black lines slashed the white canvas in all directions as if fighting each other. This impression was amplified by the red splotches of paint that marked the canvas here and there. It was titled 'Untitled no.3' on the back, and the painter's signature was illegible amid all the black lines and splashes of paint. Bob considered it very manly-looking and hung it in his study. Miranda was happy not to see it every day because it gave her nightmares.

After Bob passed away, she made his study into her own office/workplace and decorated it with framed photos from happier times, flowers and her favorite artwork. She moved the abstract painting into the living-room near the entrance, which was a room she used rarely. To her big surprise, when she had the abstract painting appraised by a reputable auction house, three experts concluded that it was an early work of the

A WALK IN THE RAIN

Spanish painter Juan Maguerrot. The estimated value was between one and two million dollars. They advised her to have it insured and to keep it in a bank safe box. She did neither because she planned to sell it and get rid of it as soon as possible. But days turned into weeks and she had so many things to do planning a life on her own, alone for the first time, that she never sold the painting.

And now it was gone.

That day started as any other in Miranda's life. Some people need a coffee early in the morning to clear their minds of sleep and help them start the day's activities. Miranda needed her early morning walk. It was that time of day when she was all by herself and she let her mind wander. It helped her a lot especially after Bob had died and she had to rethink life, being alone by herself. The morning solitary walk was as therapeutic for her as yoga meditation was for others.

The day was cold and rainy. The idea of Seattle rain as a downpour and people hurrying in the streets in a sea of umbrellas is a somewhat clichéd image. The truth is that downpours are not so frequent in Seattle. Most of the time, the rainy weather is a fine drizzle or mist. Fog is also present in this picture quite often. As for the umbrellas, these are rarely used. Seattleites wear hooded, weather-proof coats because they need their hands free to hold their purses, briefcases, bags, and the ever-present cup of coffee, the local insignia. At every street corner there is a coffee shop where people can get their favorite drink, coffee or tea, in a variety of flavors.

Miranda lived in the Magnolia neighborhood of Seattle, in an older Tudor home, which she and Bob had remodeled and updated over the years while keeping the original woodwork and character of the house. They had bought it thirty years ago when they had moved from Kansas to Seattle. Bob hoped to get a job at the Boeing Company. Instead he was offered a job at a newly started company called Microsoft. He accepted it without hesitation. He had been a senior manager on his way to an even loftier position three years ago when he died of a heart attack.

Miranda waved at Nina, the young woman

working in the flower shop. Nina was arranging some mums at the entrance of her shop. She was a cheerful sort of person, always smiling and joking. "Good morning. Want to buy a bunch of colorful mums to brighten your day? I just got them yesterday."

"Good morning Nina," Miranda answered. "Maybe I will, but I have to get a Mocha first." She pointed to the coffee shop down the road.

Nina nodded. "I would kill for a coffee myself now. My little boy was up all night fussing with a little fever. He was better and sleeping when I left, but I could use a coffee right now."

"No problem. I'll get it for you. I take my Mocha decaf. Do you want a regular latte?"

"Oh, you don't have to. I'll go for lunch and …"

"Nina, I'm going to the coffee shop anyhow. It's no problem at all."

Miranda sprinted down the road to the coffee shop. A few years ago, Billy Meyers opened a bakery. His wife was a dream baker. Her croissants and muffins were to die for and Billy was selling them faster than she could bake. He had a coffee machine and sold regular coffee to go with the baking goods, but the customers wished for a better coffee and more variety. After a year, Billy bought the retail space next door and expanded his store into a larger coffee and baking goods business that attracted a lot of people in the neighborhood.

"Hey Billy! How are you?" Miranda greeted him when she entered the store. The place was already full of people enjoying their coffee and muffins. The smell of baking was divine and the jazz music very soothing. "It was a gutsy move when you expanded the store, but I think you hit the jackpot with it." Miranda said looking around.

"That I did, Ms. Miranda. I did." Billy nodded. "Although it's a lot more work also….What can I get you? The usual Mocha decaf and a croissant?"

"Yes, please. And I want also a skinny latte, venti and two slices of your wife's cinnamon crumble coffee cake, to go. In separate bags, please." She paid for it and with her purchases returned to the flower shop.

Nina's blue eyes widened at the sight of all the

bounty Miranda deposited on her counter.

"Your latte, with caffeine. And some crumble cake fresh from Billy's wife. Here you go," Miranda said.

"I can't thank you enough." Nina got her purse from the back office.

"No, no." Miranda stopped her. "It's all on me today. I have a sad anniversary today. And I feel…" She got chocked by emotion.

Nina touched her hand. "I understand. Your husband?"

"No. Bob died in July three years ago. My daughter, my Cassidy was killed by a drunk driver fifteen years ago, this day. Life goes on, but one never recovers from losing a child." Miranda wiped her eyes, grabbed her own coffee, and turned to go.

"Wait!" Nina called after her. "I understand what you feel, I lost someone very close and dear myself…" She handed Miranda a bunch of colorful fall flowers. "I got this for you before you came back. Take them please. Flowers have a way to soothe the pain and cheer us up."

7

Miranda took the flowers, thanked Nina, and backed out of the store. She was already questioning her little breakdown and confessing to Nina her sorrow. For so many years she had borne this pain alone, rarely talking or sharing it even with Bob. Why now? And with Nina, who was a nice girl, but not a close friend. She had to acknowledge that she was lonely. After Bob's death, she had to cope with so many things alone, problems that she used to share with Bob. Then, the invitations from the couples of friends they used to socialize with dwindled, then stopped entirely after she refused some.

Now she was a fifty-nine year old woman and she was alone. She didn't know what to do with herself. She was too old to start a new career, a new relationship with another man, or a new life. But she was too young to stop living and wait to die. She was healthy with twenty or even thirty years ahead of her. What to do with all the time left? She could go to Florida to be closer to her son Bob Junior who, after a fight with his father, chose to go to college in Florida and after graduating, got a great job there as computer analyst, and decided to stay there.

A WALK IN THE RAIN

Miranda didn't share his love for the area, too hot and humid, too many insects, snakes, and alligators. Not to mention hurricanes. Junior invited her to move there permanently, but beyond all these negatives, Miranda didn't feel at home there. Maybe she was too old and set in her ways, but Puget Sound and Mt. Rainier were home to her.

~ end excerpt ~

Available from Amazon.com

34306398R00132